A DARK and COZY NIGHT

DEANNA KNIPPLING

WONDERLAND PRESS

FREE EBOOK

Get a free ebook and sign up for the Wonderland Press-Herald at wonderlandpress.com/free-fiction.

CONTENTS

WRITER'S BLOCK

It was seven p.m. on one of those June summer evenings in the Rocky Mountains that could go either way. Either the clear blue snippets of sky could join together into a clear, star-spangled night—or the clouds could squeeze tight and turn into a hailstorm banging off the hood of my 4Runner.

I didn't much care which.

My husband, Jack, had been dead just over a year. He had died on a dark and stormy evening, riding his motorcycle during a sudden rain squall. The cops had told me, from the line of rubber that he had laid down on the road, that he must have swerved out of his lane and into oncoming traffic.

Had he swerved to miss a car impatiently passing someone on the twisty mountain highway? Had he swerved to miss a deer?

I looked. There was only one skid mark on the road. Whatever he had swerved to miss hadn't even slowed down.

Afterwards, I researched how to cut brake lines and how to identify slippery, fishy-smelling brake fluid as it leaked out of an automobile. I learned the place to press on someone's neck to make them pass out—at the carotid sinus baroreceptor—and where the weakest place on someone's skull is—at the pterion.

I studied poisons, sniper rifles, drug overdoses, and, even more importantly, how to get away with all of it.

I had an excuse, though: I was, and am, a writer.

Before Jack died, I was at least hypothetically on schedule with the seventh novel in my mystery series, about a cabal of British historians who dug up the truth on historical cold cases. The seventh book was about a possible serial killer in the time of The Three Musketeers, crossed with an apparent modern-day copycat killer who had killed one of the historians. It wasn't the kind of book I could personally resist writing. I had been researching rapiers for months.

But then there was Jack, his motorcycle, and the side of a mountain, and I couldn't seem to do anything but research how a hypothetical wife of a hypothetical dead man might go about her hypothetical revenge.

My deadline came and went.

That June, I was over six months past deadline and I didn't feel any closer to putting words into my manuscript file. I was still going to conferences, though. I drank burnt-yet-under-brewed coffee and told newbie writers two correspondingly weak and bitter truths.

The first was that no matter how bad a writer was, writing wasn't a waste of time. Writing was an enrichment activity, like giving the elephants tractor tires to play with at a zoo. Creative types who don't create are at risk of going nuts. *You need to write,* I told them. *Unused gifts turn to poison.*

I didn't tell them that I was currently experiencing that poison myself.

The second truth was that the writers who were going to make it were the ones willing to put as much work into writing as a professional magician was willing to put into a card trick, not just performing the same trick over and over again—although that was part of it—but studying the magicians and tricks that had come before.

"A ten-second card trick, done well, can represent a decade of work," I told them. "Are you ready to work that hard?"

Faces glazed over, and I berated myself for thinking that I could say anything of substance to a *writer*. All I was doing was convincing the one person with talent that it wasn't worth the bother.

Other writers have the knack of sugar-coating their bitter pills. I've never learned, which was probably why I was struggling so much with the ones I had to swallow. I'd been choking over Jack's death for a year, and it still hadn't gone down.

I drove along the winding roads. The clouds were overtaking the sky.

I passed houses with dirty four-wheelers out front and kayaks hanging under their decks. I passed wood cabins and clapboard houses. I passed houses made of local rock a hundred years ago, and three-story cedar-sided modern A-frames with windows stretching from roof peak to basement. I passed hand-painted signs and satellite dishes. I passed rickety bridges over creeks, a few foolhardy final fishermen still out in their waders, silent and ghostly deer watching me from the ditches, tiny blue flowers clinging to the rocks and bobbing as the wind picked up. I drove past a fire station, a couple of churches, a gas station, an antique store, and a pizza parlor. What, after all, did I have in the fridge after being away for almost a week? I almost pulled over, but a lightning bolt close enough to leave an afterimage in my eyes and the SUV shaking from the thunder changed my mind for me: I didn't want to get caught halfway up the mountain. If a real gusher started up, the road would flood, and I'd have to head back down.

And I wanted to sleep in my own bed.

So I kept driving. A few fat splatters of rain hit the window, then stopped. Then started again, as I drove around a corner and hit a gust of wind. The SUV pulled, trying to slide into the other lane.

A bright light flashed in my eyes. A motorcyclist. I gritted my teeth and wrestled the 4Runner back where it was supposed to be, then kept driving. The rain came down hard and I turned on the wipers. Streaks of dust dragged across my vision, then washed away in the downpour. The red streak of the bike's taillight disappeared around a curve.

The rain stopped again, just to be perverse.

Why couldn't he have just pulled over and waited out the storm? Why had he kept driving? Why had he taken the bike out in the first place?

Ten minutes later, I was pulling into my driveway. There's something about me that makes me wonder if, every time I return home, I'll find the house burned to the ground. Everything seemed fine, though, except for a few places in the gravel that looked like they had been washed away in some rain. I promised myself that I'd hire a guy to bring up a load of gravel after I got the next piece of my advance.

For a book that I didn't know how to write anymore.

If I even knew how to write anymore, that was.

———

I pulled up beside the house. It was the kind of place that was perfect for Jack and me, but not that impressive compared to the neighbors'. It was a cedar-sided, two-story A-frame that had been built in the Sixties and had had one owner before us, a guy who had, after his wife's death, clung to the place like a barnacle until a broken hip had scraped him off the property and into a nursing home. We had put on a new roof and replaced the water heater, but left the old appliances in the old-fashioned galley kitchen. The floors were vinyl parquet tiles but the walls, and even the ceilings, were all natural wood. The realtor had put in new carpet in the loft and the two other bedrooms downstairs, that cheap, stinky beige stuff that sheds pieces of yarn around the edges every time you vacuum.

The built-in shelves were packed with books and knickknacks, there were two tattered old recliners in front of the wood stove, and a loft above the kitchen for a love-nest. The deck needed to be refinished, there was my office and Jack's "man cave" in the basement, and the damned driveway kept threatening to wash out completely. The finish on the table was scratched and one of the wood chairs wobbled. Jack's pots and pans still hung from their hooks, well used once but now dusty, and a chaise lounge sat in front of the big glass windows facing out over our acreage: an illusion of infinite space, with a pretty creek tinkling away at the far edge of the property. A shed on the opposite side of the house had held Jack's bike, but was empty now of all but mice and rust.

Million-dollar-plus houses surrounded us, just out of sight, but this was home.

I got out of the SUV and stopped. Something felt wrong.

I sniffed deeply, thinking that maybe a skunk had wandered through the yard, but there was nothing. A tendril of lightning snaked lazily overhead, then erupted into thunder. I took out my keys and ran for the door. I bounded up the wood steps, unlocked the door, threw myself inside, and watched a curtain of hail come battering down on the shed roof and the top of the SUV. The hail was the size of my pinkie fingernail. Nothing to worry about—yet.

I kicked off my shoes. I'd unload the SUV later. I dropped the keys on the kitchen counter, flipped on the lights, and stopped.

The kitchen had been trashed.

Cupboards open, dishes everywhere, the bottom drawer on the oven pulled out and left in the bathroom opposite the kitchen. A sour lemon-pine-vinegar-bleach smell everywhere. Soaking towels, cleaning supplies dumped out into the sink. The window had been covered with heavy black tarp and taped over with duct tape. Drawers no longer sat right on their tracks.

I went into the living room.

Books everywhere, the recliners flipped over, the wood for the stove scattered all over the floor. The curtains over the big windows at the end of the living room had been pulled closed and taped shut. So had the smaller windows. We hadn't had a TV upstairs (although there was one down in the man cave), but the stereo system had been pulled apart and left in pieces on the Persian rug, as if the thief had been interrupted.

The one thing that I needed to know was there, on top of the big wood entertainment center, was missing: a carved longhorn cow's skull, Jack's favorite possession.

Fuck.

I froze where I was, hugging myself tightly. Now was not time to panic, or explode with rage, or freak out, or curl up into a ball. Now was time to think.

My cell phone was still out in the SUV, plugged into the charger. The roof thundered with hail.

Right now, the most important thing was not "what had been stolen?" but "was the bad guy still here?"

It didn't feel like it. No cars in the driveway, for one thing, and it was a heck of a walk to a public parking area. And most of my neighbors had *NO TRESPASSING – THIS PROPERTY IS PROTECTED BY THE SECOND AMENDMENT* signs with handguns on them. You'd have to be pretty ballsy to try to park at one of their places, rather than mine, if you wanted to rob my house.

I put on my shoes in case a window was broken somewhere and did a walkthrough of the house. The windows were all closed and taped, the doors open, the drawers and closets and shelves emptied. It looked like a whirlwind had blown through.

But.

No windows were broken. The sliding doors out onto the deck hadn't been forced (and the good old low-tech wooden dowel serving as a door lock was still in place). I went back to the kitchen door and checked it. It hadn't been forced, either, and I didn't see a lot of scratch marks around the deadbolt. Presumably the ones that were there, I had put there myself.

The safe in the man cave holding Jack's guns was still in his closet, as was the safe in my closet with the titles and the social security cards. Neither had been opened. The painting in my office, a sentimental print of Leonid Afremov's *Love by the Lake,* hadn't been disturbed, and the thousand bucks in cash in the envelope behind the painting hadn't been disturbed either.

The TV in the man cave had been dumped on the floor, but it wasn't broken. Or stolen. The hard drives in both our desktop computers were still in place.

I went back up to the kitchen door and walked through the house again, this time with skeptical eyes.

Whoever had done this hadn't torn any pages out of the books. They were all over the place, but even the books that had been thrown—or placed—so that their pages were open didn't have any of the pages bent.

The stereo equipment hadn't been ripped out. Just removed and put on the floor. On top of the Persian rug. Which hadn't itself been disturbed. I mean, who trashes a house looking for something and doesn't check under the rug?

None of the trash cans had been emptied.

So someone had broken into my house without leaving a mark on either of the doors, laboriously and professionally taped up the windows, trashed the place without actually damaging anything, taken nothing of value but Jack's longhorn skull—which had been out in the open, no need for an extensive search—and left, locking the door behind them.

I wanted to untape the windows and check them for signs that someone had broken in that way, but I thought better of it: I didn't want to disturb any fingerprints, if possible. I decided that it was not possible not to make myself a cup of coffee. I also needed to pee. I used the eraser on a pencil to flush the toilet and to turn the faucets on and off, just in case.

A few minutes later I was standing in the living room with a cup of strong black coffee, working myself up to calling the cops. The roof still echoed with the constant strike of hailstones. I was going to have to drive back down the damned mountain and find a place to stay for the night after all.

I should have just stopped for pizza.

And then something terrible happened: the land line rang.

———

It was Maddy MacFarlane, a neighbor of mine, nearing eighty years of age, living in one of the million-plus homes nearby.

"Liz Hicks, home from the writers' conference. I saw your SUV pulling up into your driveway but no lights on in the house. What are you doing, standing around in the dark?"

"Hi, Maddy," I said.

"What's wrong?"

Maddy MacFarlane was as sharp as a tack, as the saying goes, or rather as sharp as a scalpel, able to cut to the point with one noncommittal comment from me and an observation about lights that didn't peep out around the window curtains.

"Someone broke in while I was out," I said.

"And?"

"And stole Jack's skull. Not *his* skull. The big carved longhorn skull on top of the entertainment center in the living room."

"I remember it," Maddy said. She had only been over to my house twice, and then only into the living room: she wasn't good with stairs anymore. But she had seen it when she was here, and commented on it: I had got it for Jack for an anniversary present the year we moved in.

Of course she remembered.

"Anything else missing?" she asked.

"Strange that you should ask," I said. "No."

"No?"

"Not that I can tell. But I've only been home—" I checked the clock on the phone; it was blinking. At some point while I was gone, the power had gone out. "Maybe half an hour. The windows have been taped up and I can't see how they got in, which tells me that it was a professional. But the cash on the back of the painting in my office is still there, and I can't see how a professional would miss that. The safes are still there, too, and they aren't bolted down or anything. The TV wasn't taken, and neither was the stereo."

Maddy said, "Liz, have you called the police yet?"

"No. I was just about to."

"Would you wait a little while?"

"Why?"

"I want you to come over here instead."

"Why?"

"To get you out of the house for the night, for one thing, but also because I have something to tell you."

"About...this?"

"I think so, yes."

"Tell me now."

"It's the sort of thing that requires time and a pot of tea, dear. A long story. You know how I've been watching the neighborhood to try to spot the burglar who's been breaking into houses?"

I blanked for a moment. Burglars in the neighborhood—and my house was the latest one to get hit up. That made sense. But when had she said anything about it? She hadn't. She'd said that she was taking up bird watching when I asked her about the powerful binoculars that I'd seen on her kitchen table a few weeks ago, though, adding that she was hearing all *sorts* of new bird calls in the neighborhoods. Then she had winked. I had assumed that she was keeping track of somebody having an affair.

If that had been a discussion about burglars in the neighborhood, it had gone completely over my head.

"Sorry, Maddy, I forgot," was what I said, though.

"It's all been over the last month," Maddy said, "And you were distracted with writing your new book, I'm sure. Deadlines, you know."

I wasn't sure whether she was teasing me or just didn't know that I was coming up empty. "Anyway?" I said.

"Any-hoo, I've gathered a bunch of us together to discuss the matter, and see if we can come to any conclusions," she said.

I shook my head. Too much was happening that night, too fast, and too *loud*: the hail was still coming down, fast and thick. "And...you're going to call us all together to expose the murderer?" I asked.

Maddy paused. "Burglar."

"Right," I said. "But, you know. Like an episode of Poirot."

"I prefer," she said, stressing the last syllable, "to think of myself as a Miss Marple. One doesn't like to admit one has a bit of an old lady mustache, even at my age. Are you coming? Or calling the cops?"

I looked around the room.

What were the police going to do? Sadly, after Jack's death I had come to realize that there were no fast, easy answers when the police were involved. It took superhuman patience to endure their form of justice. I didn't blame the police for how things had gone at Jack's death. But I couldn't exactly call them about the burglary with a light heart, knowing that they would quickly find and punish the perpetrator.

I sighed.

"I'll be right over," I said.

Card Party

But I was *not* right over. Dashing back and forth between the house and the SUV, I retrieved my belongings, dumped my dirty convention clothes out of my carry-on, and put fresh jammies and a change of clothes—ones that did *not* involve wrinkle-free polyester—back in the bag. Then I took a shower in my tiny, reassuring bathroom, washing a week of hard-water gunk buildup off me and replacing it with my favorite lavender soap, which washed off cleanly in the mountain water. I had brought a second cup of coffee into the shower with me, and drank all of it while standing under the burning, pounding stream.

By the time I got out, the hail had stopped. Good timing.

On an impulse, I grabbed my laptop bag and dumped it into the back seat of the SUV. Maybe all of this would somehow inspire me to get back to work on my novel. If nothing else, confessing to Maddy just how badly things were going would give me a guilt trip that it might be easier to write my way through than to ignore.

I put on a pair of hiking boots that weren't sweaty from being worn all day on travel, zipped myself into a waterproof shell, and ran for the SUV, locking the door behind me.

———

Maddy MacFarlane. Where do I even begin? She's a character. Born just before the Boomers started popping out of the womb in vast numbers, the tail end of the Silent Generation. Her generation didn't fight in the great wars. They endured the McCarthy years by keeping their mouths shut. They grew up relatively prosperous, believing that hard work would actually solve all their problems, but that one slip-up and they'd be back at the Great Depression.

They wore white shirts and tailored dresses. They played by the rules and earned by the work of their own two hands the fruits of the American Dream. Whenever you hear someone going off about hard work and keeping your nose clean, about how your company will do you right and pay a good pension—think Silent Generation. The ultimate conformists.

And then there was Maddy.

It wasn't hard to tell that she'd grown up in that milieu. She kept herself in shape and had perfect posture. She wore twin sets. She had Jackie O hair and wore knee-length dresses with pantyhose and pumps—eighty-year-old hips be damned. She had hatboxes. She had a calf-length plaid button-up wool coat she'd been wearing since the early Sixties. When she put out snacks for a party, she didn't stint on the anchovies or the Jell-O, and her Christmas tree was silver with a humming, rotating tri-color light to make it sparkle.

I never heard her swear, not even the day she called me after she slipped and fell on her back porch and I had to stay with her until the ambulance arrived. A broken hip, and not even one quiet *damn.* In fact, she made me get a deck of cards and we played gin rummy until the EMTs arrived.

She had been a schoolteacher. Her husband, Ed, had been a physicist working for the military. What had he invented? Sorry, that was still classified. They had made their money off *her* investments, though. She was clear about that.

Ed had died after I met her, and also after he had been moved off the mountain and down into a Denver nursing home. He had had advanced Alzheimer's. Maddy had gone to see him like clockwork, once every other week. Not more than that. Not less than that. Her nephew Nick would drive her back and forth. She claimed to not want to burden him by asking to go more often than that. I started popping over about an hour after she had gone, just to make sure she didn't sink into darkness.

"I should have killed him when I had the chance," she said once, then offered me a drink.

Her house is a one-story ranch house that looks like an architect took one look at *my* house and said, "I like it, but..." The house is bigger and wider. The siding is brown cement molded to look like wood. The door has a ramp, not stairs, and the driveway is paved—although it still gets dangerously close to being washed out on a regular basis.

The wood flooring is some kind of treated plastic, but the walls are all wood. There are no ridges between rooms, and the doors are big enough for a wheelchair, should one become required. The kitchen is modern, with mock-granite counters and wood cabinets, the kind with hardware so smooth that it is literally impossible to slam a drawer. The beige carpet is the *nice* kind that doesn't retain stains, and the bathrooms all have grab bars and padded bench seats.

The yard is landscaped, mostly with gravel, with the trees cleared away from the house. The house overlooks the same stream as my house, even though you have to back out onto the highway and take a different road to get to Maddy's place. It's literally a two-minute walk through pretty woods, in good weather, which this wasn't.

I drove, working slowly back up my driveway through a couple of inches of water, then back out to the winding road that led to about a dozen houses including mine, then back out to the highway, then back onto another road with another dozen houses, and then slowly onto Maddy's driveway and through a couple of inches of water. My stream ran past her house near the top of her driveway, normally through a culvert running under the road, then over to my house at the top of my driveway, ditto, and then flowed downhill and back again, past the bottom of my property, and then down past the bottom of Maddy's property. That's how close we were.

On the way over, I checked my phone. New message from Maddy. She had called my cell trying to find me. Presumably, when she hadn't reached me, she had tried the house.

At the end of Maddy's driveway were a number of cars. And several motorcycles. Not *exactly* enough for a motorcycle gang, but still a fair number. The bikes were in the open garage, the cars parked between the garage and the house. In the garage was a young man, I want to say about twenty or twenty-five years old. I gave him a second look, but it wasn't Nick, Maddy's nephew, or, rather, great-nephew. Nick was tall and gangly and awkward looking, not unhandsome per se. A young Boris Karloff with a pencil mustache, more than anything else. I didn't know much about him, other than that his parents were both dead, and that Maddy's sister was kind of, well, a bitch, so Maddy had become his adoptive mentor and grandmother, as it were.

This was someone else, someone shorter, with a goatee. He stopped working on the bike—it wasn't Nick's, which was red—and watched me find a place to park around the edge of the driveway.

I picked a spot under an old pine tree and hoped for the best, grabbing my carry-on and the laptop bag and running for the house. A splatter of rain hit me in the face as I passed the garage, more to remind me of the storm than anything else, I think. I made it to the front door, which opened as I approached it, revealing Nick, who held the door for me as I rushed inside.

"Thanks, Nick."

"No problem. Sorry Jack's skull got stolen."

Maddy must have told him already. "Me, too," I said. "But hey. It sounds like your aunt has the solution to the whodunnit in hand already."

Nick put a finger to his lips and jerked his head toward the rest of the house. "She's not sure yet," he cautioned.

"Right, right," I said. "Wait for the big reveal."

Normally, when someone burgles a whole neighborhood—and does so in such a professional manner—there are professionals, plural, involved. There are plenty of professional thieves in Denver. They hit neighborhoods on rotation like bandits raiding villages after a harvest: you have to wait until the victims have recovered from the last time you've hit them, or there won't be anything worth stealing.

The ones I've heard about, though, mostly just sweep through the neighborhood stealing cars, riffling through glove boxes, and only breaking into empty houses with FOR SALE signs out front. I'd never had to write about anyone breaking into multiple houses in one neighborhood. Most of the time, a burglary is performed on a single house by a male under twenty-five who has been in the house before. It's a case of "you have stuff, why shouldn't I?" Most burglaries are strictly amateur hour.

In other words, not people who know to tape up the windows and avoid leaving break-in marks on the doors. And they don't hang around long enough to trash an entire house...and they *definitely* don't leave expensive stereo equipment behind.

It had to be a professional.

And yet it couldn't be a professional, if they had hit up multiple houses in the neighborhood, over the course of a month. Some of my neighbors had serious security systems, high-tech, with alarms that would trigger a call to the police if the system wasn't shut down properly.

"Who's the motorcycle gang?" I asked.

"Friends, mostly," he said. "We all went out this morning thinking it was going to be good weather. Nana said she wanted some noise in the house, let's have a barbecue. Ate too much. Everyone lolled around playing board games and didn't notice the storm coming in."

"Is there room for everyone?" I tried to remember how many bikes had been in the garage. More than four, less than ten? "Should I go back home?"

"All good. We have air mattresses and couches in the basement."

"Whoa," I said. "There's a basement? I didn't even know."

He grinned at me. "Dude who built the house was a prepper."

"There's a *bomb shelter* under the house? And Maddy never told me?"

"Dunno. Something. Show you the door later. It's cool."

Maddy was waving at me from the kitchen-slash-living room, a large open space scattered with rugs and chairs and coffee tables. The oak dining room table, which had been stretched out to its full length, was strictly for playing cards and games and snacks, as far as I'd ever seen.

"Yoo hoo, Liz! Over here! Nick, don't be so selfish. Send her over here."

I looked around the side of the door to see whether it was a "shoes off" or "shoes on" day. A few pairs of shoes lay on the rubber mat, most of them too big to be Maddy's. I kicked mine off, glad I had changed into clean socks.

It was a strange assortment of guests. Besides Nick, there were another two young men of his age sitting on a leather couch, passing a legal pad between them and snorting like two middle-schoolers passing dirty notes. I recognized the others: Marianne and Jim Griffiths, two Army retirees that I thought had gone on, or might have just come back from, vacation; Robert DeFoor, a computer programmer who had worked on my computer a couple of times since Jack's death as a favor; and Sally Strobridge, who was a real estate agent and the neighborhood gossip, the kind of woman who submits the "neighborhood news" to the weekly local newspaper. Your business is her business.

I waved at everyone and called a hello, then joined Maddy at the kitchen island, where she was cutting up veggies for a crudités platter. She was carving radishes into a variety of flowers to add to the center of the platter, along with her tomato roses, cucumber leaves, and carrot blossoms. She had her silver-gray hair back under a kerchief and was wearing a red print dress with tiny white flowers under a pink apron covered with cats. She even had lipstick on. I smelled puff pastry cooking in the oven.

"Fancy," I said.

"One so seldom has an opportunity to make garnishes," she said, then sniffed. "*You* never really appreciate them. Nick doesn't either."

"Nick's all right," I said.

She sighed. "He's at a troublesome age. He needs to get married and settle down."

I laughed, not sure why what she'd said was so funny. "I just don't see a white picket fence in Nick's future. How is everything *else* going?"

Maddy made a face, and suddenly she looked her age. "Rotten," she said. "*So* far. But let's not talk about that now."

"Is there anything you want me to do?"

"You *are* a mystery writer," she said. "If you could just solve the mystery for me, that would be nice."

"Not a clue?" I said.

"Better if you get your own clues," said Maddy, smiling. "Coffee? Whiskey? Coffee with whiskey? What can I do you for?"

I opted for an Irish coffee and dosed it myself lightly with Tullamore Dew. As soon as I had noisily slurped it, suddenly everyone else felt like having one, and I found myself making several.

"Do you have decaf?" Marianne asked. Sally wanted skim milk. One of Nick's friends wanted soy milk and no whipped cream—which just went to show that a man could have tattoos from wrist to neck and still be vegan. Nick's friends' names were Egan and Tony, and the guy outside was Austin. Egan was the tattooed vegan (easy enough to remember), and Tony had a tiger tattoo on his shoulder. I resisted the urge to tell him about the Frosted Flakes mascot. *Deeee-licious.* I didn't want him to think I was hitting on him, or, worse, making the same dumb joke about his name that he'd heard fifty times already.

Don't be middle-aged, I reminded myself. *Remember that you, too, once thought black leather pants were cool.*

I had just served everyone with fresh drinks (and discovered that mine had gone cold) when Nick's friend Austin came in through the back door.

"All done?" Nick called.

Austin spouted out some incomprehensible car talk that I took to mean, "that one thing was being stubborn but I showed it who was boss."

Nick nodded in approval, then pointed at me. "Ask the lady to give you a drink. Irish Coffee. They're good."

I don't think I'll ever get used to being called a *lady*. I mentally insert *old* in front of the word every time I hear it. But I made Austin his drink, then dumped mine out and started it again.

Just as I was about to take a sip, there came a knock at the door.

The Percentage of Cheaters

"Who is it?" called Maddy, who had carried the crudités platter to the table, and was taking snapshots of her knife work on her phone. Quickly, I took a deep drink of my Irish coffee, getting whipped cream all over my upper lip. I was *not* going to spend all day playing bartender. The door opened to a flash of lighting and the face of a woman I recognized: Wendy Smith. My house cleaner.

The houses on my stretch of the mountains included everything from trailer houses to million-dollar mansions. Wendy lived in one of the former. She was a native Coloradan who had literally seen a million people move into Denver, and the mountain go from "the backwoods" to "a good place for luxury McMansions."

She was one of those women with round faces and broad smiles that look like their true calling in life was to be a Medieval barmaid. She had long brown hair with straight-cut bangs and wore a tan trench coat streaming with water, and was carrying an overnight bag.

"Hey, Maddy," she said, tiredly.

"What is it, honey?"

"Tree fell on my house, knocked out the power, and tore a hole through my roof," Wendy said, in the same tone of voice someone might use to explain that they had a flat tire on the way to work.

"Oh, sweetie," Maddy said, rushing over. "Do you need a place to stay?"

"It looks like you're full up."

"Nonsense. You'll take the left-hand guest room. The boys are taking the—" Maddy winked— "*basement.* And everyone else will be going home for the night."

Wendy sighed, letting her shoulders sink with relief. "Oh, thank you." She hung up her coat on the overcrowded coat rack and slipped off her shoes at the mat, then walked through the kitchen, grinning at the guests in the living room, and disappeared down the hallway to the rest of the house.

From his easy chair in the living room, Jim Griffiths cleared his throat and called over his shoulder, "You might end up with more guests than you expected, Mads."

"Oh?"

"Marianne and I rode over here on the bikes. I think it's too wet to ride back home tonight."

I said, "Oh, I can give you a ride back home in the 4Runner."

Marianne smiled at me. "Thank you, Elizabeth."

I didn't like Jim and Marianne. The only reason I'd offered was so Maddy didn't have to put up with them all night. It was hard to put a finger on exactly why I didn't like them.

They'd never done anything to me; they'd never treated me with anything less than respect. But there it was: I didn't like them, and never had.

Jim was one of those people with a long, manly sort of face and a crooked nose. A man's man. He carried himself with restraint and grace, but no real intelligence or wit. Maybe it was just that he never laughed at my dry jokes, when we ran into each other at a convenience store or at the pizza place. It was like trying to crack a joke at a Gila monster.

Marianne was one of those women who live their lives blankly, barely registering anything going on around them, keeping a blank smile on their faces as long as anyone might be looking. For a while, I'd try to catch the look on her face when she didn't think anyone was looking at her, but it was a lost cause. Either her face was stuck or she just assumed that someone was looking at her *all* the time, whether she could see them or not. Short, dyed red hair with an Eighties wave to it, plucked eyebrows, lavender and teal eye makeup, darker lip liner than her lipstick, signs of having been over-tanned at a tanning booth over the decades. She was a fan, though, so I couldn't exactly be too harsh on her: she liked John Grisham, Scott Turow, Martin Cruz Smith, Len Deighton, Tom Clancy, Robin Cook. She didn't care for cozies or anything too deep, like John le Carré. It had steamed me at first: someone who didn't like le Carré liked my books. What did that say about my writing? But oh well. At least she read books, and liked mine. I liked to think that she was constantly imagining herself in an alternate reality where she was secretly in deep cover for the KGB.

"Time for cards!" Maddy exclaimed.

"Oh, good, time for bridge," said Sally, standing up from her seat.

"Not bridge, cribbage," said Maddy, cheerfully ignoring the way Sally's thin smile fell. "The boys don't know bridge, and I don't like to drop them in the deep water with the sharks."

Sally sniffed, pressing her lips together, but lifted her chin, and took a seat at the dining room table. "We could teach them."

"Or we could play poker," Austin said earnestly. "I could teach you how to play Texas Hold 'Em, if you don't know how. Penny a point."

Maddy said, "Don't teach grandma to suck eggs, Austin!"

Sally yelped out loud: "I'm only fifty-three!" while Austin said, "Suck eggs?" and I snorted into my Irish coffee. Sally was sixty-five if she was a day.

"Mansplaining to your elders," I translated for Austin's sake. "I think I'm the only one of the oldsters who doesn't take a two-week vacation in Vegas every year to pad out the retirement fund. In short, watch your ass."

Bob DeFoor, who had seemed uncomfortably quiet since I'd arrived, said, "I count my cards in Atlantic City. I know too many people in Vegas."

Austin chewed on the inside of his cheek and dropped into the chair next to Sally's.

"Teams?" I asked, mentally counting heads: Mickey, Egan, Austin, and Tony the Tiger, plus Maddy, myself, Sally, Bob, Marianne, and Jim. Ten was a lot of bodies for cribbage, even with two teams.

Wendy came back into the room, a stiff, friendly grin still plastered on her face. Which made eleven.

Marianne said, "I'd rather not play. We've had a lot of riding lately, and I'd like to just relax, please."

"Of course," Maddy said.

Nick said, "I'm out. Be your dogsbody."

"I'm your huckleberry," Tony said in a Southern drawl, quoting Val Kilmer in *Tombstone.*

Bob suddenly jumped in with, "Does this mean we're not friends anymore? You know, if I thought you weren't my friend, I don't think I could bear it."

Jim looked at everyone blankly as we all chuckled. Austin said, "What's a dogsbody?" then looked at me.

"Unpaid intern," I said, and we all laughed.

Maddy said, "Liz, I hereby designate you the official inter-generational translator for the evening. Two of the boys in one group but not on the same team."

"I pick *her*," Austin said, pointing at Sally.

Maddy said, "She might be a shark, Austin, but nobody ever said she was the *biggest* shark in the waters tonight."

I said, "Sorry, Maddy, I'm just not up for cards tonight." And which left eight players even.

"Oh? Are you all right?"

I blinked, thinking that it should have been obvious that I wasn't all right, because I'd already told her that I'd been robbed...then I remembered that I was supposed to be playing along with whatever her plan was.

And now was the time to bring up the subject.

I said, "Someone broke into my house while I was gone."

A few minutes later, we had established that I hadn't called the cops yet and that everyone but the boys, Wendy, and Maddy had had their places broken into over the last month. Jim and Marianne's place had been hit on Friday, May thirty-first; Bob's on Tuesday, June fourth; and Sally's on Wednesday, June fifth. Each place had been selectively, intelligently ransacked: cash, electronic equipment, expensive tools, and, in Sally's case, some expensive gemstone jewelry, and also the kind of paperwork that could give an identity thief all the material they needed to steal your identity: tax returns, social security cards, sheets full of passwords...

"Wait," I said, "didn't you guys have all that stuff in a safe?"

The safes had been opened. Mine hadn't, but I didn't say that.

Bob DeFoor clarified the situation a little by saying, ruefully, "We all had WiFi enabled safes and security systems. It's no big mystery. Whoever got in, hacked their way in."

"What security system do you have?" Jim asked.

"Not as sophisticated as whatever you have, I'm sure," I said. I didn't feel like telling him I didn't have one, or enduring the lecture I'm sure he would have given me. "It looks like the burglar went through it like a hot knife through butter. I didn't even have a clue that something was wrong until I unlocked the door."

Bob said, "And of all people, I was the one who should have known better."

"How so?" I asked politely.

His face turned a little red. "I'm a security consultant. It is literally my *job* to tell people that no matter how secure they think their security system is, if someone is determined enough, they'll be able to break in."

I had heard the same sentiment before: there was no such thing as unpickable lock, and never had been. Security theater. The general idea was just to make the effort required to break into a place so off-putting that thieves just picked somewhere else to break into.

Maddy said, "That's not true. What about Fort Knox?"

Bob said, "I worked out how to do it, once. For fun. But, honestly, people are so caught up in the idea of it being Fort Knox that nobody even bothers."

"That you know of," I said. "The government controls the place. If anyone *had* broken into Fort Knox and stolen something, do you think they'd announce it?"

"You don't really think they would cover up something like that?" Jim said, deprecatingly.

I tapped the side of my nose. He snorted and turned toward the pair of cribbage boards that Maddy had laid out on the table. She opened a kitchen drawer and pulled out two decks of Bicycle cards, both decks still wrapped, and tossed them to Bob and Jim.

Nick said, "Aw, Maddy. Wrapped decks? Seriously?"

"Fifty percent of all Monopoly players cheat," Maddy said. "A quarter of people are cheaters and another quarter of people will go along with a cheater if someone else starts it. There are four players for each cribbage board. You do the math." Then she stuck her tongue out at him. "Honestly, kids these days."

"Who's the cheater in my group?" Austin asked.

Maddy said, "If you think that anyone in this room wouldn't cheat at cards, given the chance, then you're being naïve. The non-cheaters have self-selected themselves out of this group."

"Really?" He looked around at the table. "Uh...so Liz and Marianne aren't cheaters? I know Nick's a cheater."

Nick raised his hands, palms out. "I try to use my powers for good."

Jim said, "Marianne's not a cheater. She's sharp, though, when you can get her to play."

Maddy said, "Liz is the one to watch. She'll watch you cheat all night, then come up to you later and thank you for demonstrating how to double-deal."

I rolled my eyes. Just because I'd caught Maddy at it once didn't give me superpowers. Nevertheless, the others looked at me speculatively.

"Did she blackmail you?" Sally asked.

Maddy laughed. "Not yet!"

I said, "And Wendy is honest, of course."

Wendy looked straight into my eyes, and said, "I try. I'm not perfect, though."

"Name one time that you haven't been honest," Jim demanded.

Wendy's face turned red. "It's not that big of a deal."

"Come on, spit it out!"

"I...don't always write down mileage on my cleaning trips, so sometimes I have to guess for my taxes."

Jim burst out in a big guffaw. "You're pulling my leg!"

Wendy stood up from the table, looking as if she were near tears. "Excuse me." And fled down the hallway. Maddy gave me a look, and I followed Wendy down the hallway.

She had closed the guest room door behind her.

I knocked quietly. "Wendy? It's me, Liz."

Just then guffaws of laughter broke out in the other room, and I couldn't hear if she made any response. But the door cracked open and Wendy peeked out, a tear streak down the side of her face.

"Oh," she said. Then, hoarsely, she whispered, "Liz? You need to see this."

She opened the door wider.

Inside the room, half-covered by a printed cotton sheet, was Jack's longhorn skull.

In the Guest Room

The guest room was homey, but not *too* homey. A large, wood-paneled room with two full-sized beds in it, both of them made up with plain white quilts, baby-blue knit blankets, and a stack of pillows that stretched halfway down the beds. The floor had a Native-style blue and white blanket on a backing. The walls held no family photographs, but a few pieces of eclectic Southwestern-style art: bright knitted burros, a silver motorcycle bookend on a simple white dresser surrounding a few coffee-table books on Georgia O'Keeffe, three rattan goat heads with horns on the wall next to the closet.

The longhorn skull was in a corner between the wall and the foldout closet door. The sheet covering it was thrown back, as if Wendy had just discovered it. Her large leather satchel rested on the rug, and the top drawer of the dresser was opening, revealing a few rolled-up pieces of clothing—Maddy kept extra pajamas and socks and things for unexpected visitors.

"Isn't this supposed to be at your house?" Wendy asked. Her smile had stretched a bit thin.

"Yes," I said.

Wendy bit her lips for a second. Then: "This wasn't here the last time I cleaned Maddy's house."

"When was that?"

"June sixth, about eleven in the morning."

It was the eleventh, a Tuesday. June sixth would have been the Thursday before that. I had left for the conference on the sixth at about eight a.m. to go to the airport for my flight. Wendy had last cleaned my house on June third, a Monday. I reserve Mondays for running errands, entering receipts, answering emails, and general business tasks. When I'm writing, that is. Mostly on Mondays lately I had been driving down the mountain and walking around parks and shopping malls in Denver, going out to lunch with other writers, killing time.

"And you didn't happen to go back into my house while I was gone?"

"No, of course not."

I believed her.

"And you didn't happen to see anything strange happening in the neighborhood over the next few weeks?" I asked.

"You're taking this pretty calmly," Wendy said.

"I've become quite good at shutting down my emotions when I run into something unpleasant," I said.

Wendy frowned and shook her head. "That's probably not a good thing."

"You're not wrong," I admitted. "But have you seen anything strange lately?"

She screwed up her face, tilted her head to the side—then turned around and threw the sheet back over the skull. Good idea. She said, "I'll think about it. A lot of motorcycles in the area, but that's not actually unusual in the summer. I haven't seen any strange cars parked at anyone's houses or heard any rumors of someone looking for a carved longhorn skull, if that's what you're asking."

I snorted. "No trail of breadcrumbs."

"What are you going to say to Maddy?" Wendy asked. "You know that Nick and his friends are in trouble, don't you?"

"Do you think it's them?"

"Well," Wendy said. "On motorcycles? Probably not."

I considered the big skull and how awkward it would be to ride with it. I'd never driven a motorcycle myself, but I'd ridden on the back of Jack's bike plenty of times. Awkward didn't cover it, and it would have stuck out like a sore thumb. You're never quite as solitary out on our mountain as you feel like you are.

"What happened with Nick and his friends?"

"I know that he's been kicked out of his parents' house," Wendy said. "He's been living in the basement at Maddy's for a month now."

"And *why* have I never heard about this basement?" I exclaimed.

Wendy smiled, this time a sly little smirk. "Maddy made me promise never to talk about it with someone who didn't know."

"She didn't tell me," I grumped.

"She doesn't like to tell *anyone*."

"Where's the door?"

"If you haven't found it on your own, I'm not going to tell you," Wendy said primly.

I took a breath. Curiosity killed the cat...and could derail an interrogation. "What else do you know about Nick?"

"Just that the cops are involved somehow," Wendy said. "He got a phone call while I was cleaning. It was from his *lawyer*."

I blinked. Getting a call from a lawyer didn't necessarily involve the police, but maybe Wendy had heard a snippet or two of the conversation that implied it. Not something I wanted to press her on, though: I'd be better off asking Maddy or Nick.

"How long have Nick's friends been here?"

"Just yesterday and today, I think," Wendy said. I didn't ask how she knew. I couldn't think of a way to ask that wouldn't make it sound like I suspected her story.

I didn't think she had stolen the skull, even though she had a key to the house, let alone brought it over to Maddy's house and hid it clumsily in the guest room even though there was a perfectly good bomb shelter basement to hide it in. It didn't make sense. Why show me?

Or had it not been *Wendy* who wanted to show me the skull, but Maddy?

Maddy had told Wendy to take this bedroom. Wendy was impossibly honest. Wendy would show me the skull, if I didn't find it on my own (I was nosy; one or the other was bound to happen). Therefore, Maddy knew that I would see the skull. She probably knew that I was seeing it now. Maddy had, in fact, encouraged me with her look to follow Wendy down the hall.

Was Maddy trying to tell me that Nick had stolen the skull?

Why would Nick steal something from my *house*, then bring it *here*, and then, again, knowing about the basement, leave it in the guest room?

I didn't think Maddy was strong enough to carry the skull any distance. Therefore: I didn't think Maddy had stolen the skull, and I didn't think she had moved the skull from a hidden basement to the guest room.

I shook my head. It was almost spinning anyway. "I don't know what to think," I told Wendy.

"Me, either. I just don't want you to think that I did it."

"I don't think you did," I said.

"And I didn't steal anything from anyone else's house, either," she said. Her face had turned red. I had been so involved in my own thoughts that I hadn't noticed.

I hesitated. "I don't want you to take this the wrong way, because I believe you, but can you prove that? To the police?"

"No," Wendy said. Tears rose in her crystal blue eyes. "I don't think so."

"Wendy, did a tree really fall on your house?" I asked, a sudden guess.

Her shoulders slumped. In a tiny voice, she said, "No. Maddy told me to say it."

I bellowed with laughter, quickly clapping my mouth shut and suppressing the gaudy noise before it could carry into the conversation outside the room.

"You did *great* lying to everyone," I said. "I didn't even think twice about it. But it is sort of strange that only people who have been burgled are here tonight...and then you show up. I think Maddy is trying to prove your innocence."

Maddy had already told me most of it, but I was amused that I hadn't put it together with Wendy's appearance.

Wendy nodded. "Yes, that was supposed to be the plan. But I just don't see how it's supposed to happen."

"I don't know either," I said, even though I had a suspicion of what Maddy was up to. "But let's play along with it and try to help her."

"I don't want anything bad to happen," Wendy said. Then she corrected herself: "I don't want anything bad to happen to *Maddy*," she said.

I could only agree.

PLAYING ALONG

We emerged from the room, Wendy a bit red-eyed, but nobody seemed to take note: she had rushed off in an upset only a few moments ago, after all.

The two games of cribbage were under way. The kitchen side of the table, which had been pulled away from the island, held Sally and Austin as partners, with Bob and Tony playing opposite them. So far, Sally and Austin were slightly ahead at about sixty points. Bob and Tony were quoting movies at each other:

"Go ahead. Make my day," Bob said.

"Face it, girls. I'm older and I have more insurance," Tony replied.

I rolled my eyes. How they had figured each other out so quickly, I didn't know: but a lot of partnered cribbage relies on what cards you suspect the other players have. Knowing the kinds of cards your partner has is invaluable...especially when it comes to the one card you have to discard into the crib, or "extra" hand that gets counted for points at the end of each round. It was Bob's crib, and his points at the end of the round.

Bob had just told Tony that he was putting a five in the crib—his quote was five words long. Tony had just responded that he was throwing in a ten with his ten-word quote, which would give Bob an automatic two points.

At the living room side of the table were Maddy partnered with Egan, and Jim partnered with Nick. Wendy's flight to the guest room had left an open place at the table for Nick to fill.

Jim kept looking into the living room at Marianne, but she didn't seem to be the least bit interested: she was already lost in a book.

I watched Maddy's group play for a few moments, my mind trying to grasp the discovery of the skull. The only thing that I could come up with was that my house had been burgled, and Maddy had found out who it was, and had Nick break in and steal the skull and put it in the guest room...but that didn't make sense, either. Why not just put it back where it belonged and leave me a note?

Maddy winked at me.

Jim said, pointedly, "People who aren't playing shouldn't stand behind people who are."

I said, "Excuse me," and moved away from the table.

Jim and Nick were losing, twenty points to forty, and, as I watched, Egan concluded a seven-eight-nine run with a six: "Run of four, fifteen two."

Jim's face, already red, turned redder. "Damn it, Nick, you don't lay down a seven first thing! At least have the decency to have a one. To make up thirty-one."

Nick said, "Nope."

Maddy said, "I've got it! Thirty-one for two."

It didn't bode well for the Jim-Nick partnership. It didn't bode well at all.

As Nick shuffled, Maddy said, "So, Egan, do you have a girlfriend?"

My ears pricked up. Egan said, "Nope."

"Seeing anyone?"

"Sort of."

"Who?"

Egan's eyes slid toward Jim. "I have a boyfriend. He lives down in Denver."

Jim rolled his eyes. *Kids these days.* But the moment passed, and both I and Egan relaxed visibly.

"Oh!" Maddy said. "I should have asked a better question the first time. Sometimes you trip over your own nosey nose."

"Don't worry about it," Egan said.

Nick dealt, and they considered their cards. Wendy said, "Would anyone like anything to drink?"

The Irish coffees were gone. Jim wanted a Scotch, the boys all asked for soft drinks out of the fridge, in a way that showed that they all knew what types of soda were already in there, Bob cleared his throat and asked for "something with more caffeine," and Sally seconded him, but asked that it be decaf. Maddy pursed her lips and said she wanted a gimlet.

"With or without a little soda?"

"With."

I shook my head, and Marianne requested "whatever kind of tea you have, any type is fine, really."

I helped Wendy pass out the drinks while the two tables played.

"So *tell* me about your boyfriend," Maddy said to Egan.

"He likes bad sweaters," Egan said. "And puffer jackets. He gets a haircut like twice a month at a *barber* shop."

"Any tattoos?" Maddy asked.

"Not a one," Egan said sadly.

"How long have you been together?"

"Three years."

"I thought it would have been longer," Maddy said. "You look like a seven-year man. Or a ten-year one."

"Three," Egan said firmly.

"Any dogs?" Maddy asked.

"Lou has one," Egan said. "It's ten years old."

"Just the one?"

"He's been thinking about getting another one."

"Two dogs is a lot, for two people who have only been together three years."

"You might think that."

The penny dropped, and I realized that they, too, were discussing their hands. A few seconds later, they had trapped Nick and Jim into giving up more points—using twos, threes, and tens. Maddy also had an ace to cap things off for a thirty-one.

Of the two strategies, I liked the quotes better: after a while, talking about numbers of things was sure to get Maddy and Egan busted. But not this time.

I grabbed a stool at the kitchen island and a plate of crudités, then considered the question at hand. Not "who stole Jack's longhorn skull," but "who has been burgling houses?"

What I knew: that Sally's, Jim and Marianne's, Bob's, and my house had all been professionally burgled. And that Wendy cleaned for all of those houses, and that Sally had been the realtor for all of them (even herself). I knew those things based on casual conversation with Maddy, rather than a conversation as a group. I wasn't sure if everyone knew, or if everyone knew that everyone knew. Presumably everyone that at least some of the others used Wendy to clean, and had used Sally as their realtor.

I also knew the dates of the burglaries: May thirty-first (Jim and Marianne), June fourth (Bob), and June fifth (Sally). I knew roughly what was stolen—or at least what everyone *said* was stolen—which were normal, ordinary things of value, and paperwork that could be used for identity theft.

We all knew each other, and we all knew Maddy.

What I didn't know: who stole the material. Whether it was the same person in each of the cases or not. Whether anyone had helped anyone else. *Why* anything had been stolen?

What I could pretty easily assume: that, because our neighborhood was so isolated, whoever had done the burglaries had had inside knowledge. High-grade security systems had been bypassed, no strangers had been spotted at each other's houses, and an intimate knowledge of people's schedules had been suggested.

Should I assume an insider was involved? Or was it really a case of a professional burglary team?

Another option might be that an actual burglary team had hit a house or two, and then another house had been hit up in a similar way, for insurance purposes. Or were my neighbors all in a conspiracy of insurance losses? That would be a new one. I searched around the kitchen floor. My keys were in my pocket, but my phone was still in my SUV, along with my purse. I was being a real space case. I found a sticky note and wrote "A conspiracy to commit insurance fraud?" on it and shoved it in the same pocket as the keys. Behind me, Wendy was cleaning up Maddy's mess in the kitchen.

"Whatcha thinking?" asked Maddy.

Was this my cue to start asking people questions about their burglaries? Probably.

"I'm trying to decide whether I'm mad enough to call the cops," I said.

"You haven't called them yet?" Jim asked.

Oops. I'd forgotten to come up with a story about why I hadn't before I'd spouted that out. "No," I said. "I was so upset when I got home that I didn't. I would have just screamed at whoever answered the phone."

For some reason, that seemed to make sense to him. He said, "You seem calmer now."

"But how long am I going to spend on hold?" I said. "And how much do I want to be making this call in front of other people, anyway?"

"Sooner is better," Jim said pointedly.

"What did *you* do?" I asked. "You were burgled on the thirty-first, right? Weren't the two of you supposed to be on vacation or something? Was it while you were out of town?"

"Yes," Jim said.

Egan asked, "Can you even go on vacation if you're retired?"

I rolled my eyes. "That's like asking if you can go on vacation if you're self-employed."

"Sor-ry," Egan said.

"We both do a lot of volunteering," Jim said. "Lots of things for church, Habitat for Humanity, the Pediatric Brain Tumor Foundation—anywhere that needs us, really."

Egan's face softened a little. "That's cool. Sorry I made a rude assumption."

Jim said, proudly, "That's all right. You're young."

Egan opened his mouth, closed it again.

"But when was the burglary?" I asked.

"We went to Vegas on..." Jim frowned. "Marianne? What day did we leave for Vegas?"

Without looking up, she called, "May the twenty-eighth. Tuesday. We stayed at the Aria on the Strip."

I looked back toward Jim and caught him pressing a mark into the edge of a card with his thumbnail. His shuffle was up next, and I watched as he double-dealt cards with real smoothness. Maddy's back was to me, so I couldn't see her reaction, but I doubted that she had missed it. Had he been double-dealing the whole time? I wasn't sure. I wished I'd been paying better attention.

Nick's profile didn't show any special reaction.

"How did you do in Vegas?" Maddy asked pleasantly.

"We just about broke even," Jim said. "Maybe a little ahead."

"That's good," she said. "I don't dare go, myself. I'd be too tempted to cheat a little. How would that look, an old lady like me getting busted for cheating! I have no doubt that the security crews in Vegas are better at picking up on that kind of thing than I would be at getting away with it!"

Nick said, "You do *not* cheat at cards, Aunt Maddy."

Maddy reached over and patted the back of his hand. "Let's just leave it that way, shall we?"

Jim said, "I don't need to cheat. I have a system."

"Is it a good one?" Egan asked.

"You might not think so," Jim said, "because I didn't win a million bucks. But every time you break even, you're doing well—because the house takes a cut of the winnings, so it's harder to get ahead, or even make back your losses."

Egan nodded. "You have to be smarter than the dealer."

"It's more complicated than that," Jim said dismissively. "But it's a good system. Could be better. But good enough. I won't go into any details, though, so don't ask."

I struggled to remember something on the tip of my tongue. "Weren't you doing something else there, too?" I had run into the two of them at the local grocery store at some point earlier in May, I couldn't remember exactly when. Or what we talked about. I just remember that Vegas was involved somehow.

"We went to a motocross race," Jim said. "An exhibition race, not part of the official Supercross races. A charity race."

"Did you ride all the way to Vegas?" I asked.

It doesn't sound like a long drive to Las Vegas from Colorado, but in fact it was a twelve-hour ride, or longer if you wanted to enjoy the scenery—and most cyclists do.

"We have friends in Vegas who loaned us their bikes," Jim said. "We rode in a couple of races but didn't place in anything. Marianne got a recognition award for raising money. We flew down."

He looked pointedly at me; I couldn't remember what the charity was, but I *had* turned them down when I ran into them in the grocery store.

The deal had come back around to Maddy; I watched her smooth a mark on one of the cards, so that it would be harder for Jim to find it the next time he dealt or cut.

From the other side of the table, Austin said, "And that makes thirty-one."

Bob and Tony groaned. I glanced over as Austin placed the final peg at the end of the board. It had been a close game: the other pegs were all clustered together near the end.

Sally said, "It's all a matter of watching your opponent. 'Go ahead. Make my day' indeed."

She had, of course, caught on to the boys' cheating. Austin guffawed. Either he had also caught on, or he'd found another way to signal.

Maddy stretched from side to side. The game they were playing looked to have a *bit* more of a spread from the last peg to the first one, and, if she played her cards correctly, she and Egan should leave Jim and Nick behind at the skunk line.

I wondered if she would deliberately play a little worse, and let Jim slip past that humiliating mark on the board, or trounce him for the pleasure of humiliating him.

Sally said, "Best of three or switch teams?"

"Let's wait until they're done," Austin said.

Maddy didn't *seem* to give any signal I could catch to Egan, but the two of them played a little weaker during the last few hands, and Jim and Nick were able to scrape by before Maddy pegged out on a hand full of sevens and eights.

"Well, that's that!" she announced, reaching over to Jim to shake his hand. "A fair fight."

He grinned at her.

I wasn't sure if he was proud of not getting caught cheating, or planning something worse next round.

"Well?" Sally asked. "Switch it up or keep playing it straight?"

"Switch it up," Maddy announced. "How are these whipper-snappers supposed to learn, otherwise? If you stay with the same players, you learn how to defeat that player—not the cards."

Egan said, "You can never defeat the cards. What's fate is fate."

My throat tightened, and I turned my head to the side.

As though she understood exactly what was on my mind, Wendy said from behind me, "That's like saying there's no point in learning how to play cards, Egan. Because if every card has already been fated, why bother?"

Egan took a breath to start explaining to Wendy why that was fated, too—when Maddy put a hand on his arm. "Because sometimes even Fate cheats, Egan."

"Let it go," Nick growled. Egan nodded.

Wendy brought out another tray of veggies—the first one had been nearly demolished. The smell of puff pastry rose in the air; she must have thrown something in the oven while I wasn't paying attention.

"As soon as these spinach puffs come out of the oven," she said, "I'll take over for Nick."

The Basement

"So," Bob said. "Where is this famous secret basement? When was it built?"

"It's a secret," Maddy announced. "I have a rule. No one gets to tell anyone how to find or get into the basement. You can figure it out—or you can spy on someone who already knows, which is, I believe, how the rest of the boys figured it out. They were on a deadline, though, if they didn't want to sleep on the living room floor tonight."

"Couldn't they have used the guest room?" Sally asked. "You weren't planning on having Wendy come over, that was just a strange freak of the storm."

"I told them they had to be out of the guest room by tonight, because if any of *you* wanted to spend the night—you know how suddenly storms come up—they had to be ready to give up their room," Maddy said.

"But—"

I said, "She just told them that to push them to find it, no doubt."

Sally sniffed.

"Who knows how to find the basement door?" I asked.

"No one is going to tell you, so don't even ask!" Maddy said.

"I didn't say I was going to ask!" I exclaimed, laughing. "I just want to know who knows!"

Maddy said, "I know, Nick and the boys know, and everyone else who knows is dead. D-E-A-D dead!" Then she laughed. "Except for the builder. I think he still knows. But the previous owner has passed."

"*I* know," Marianne said from her big comfy chair in the living room.

"You do?" Maddy said, surprised.

"I've known for a while."

"Where is it?" Jim demanded.

Marianne looked up from her book, her face looking tired for a moment, her short, dyed-red hair falling over one eye. She brushed it back. A small smile crossed her lips. "I'm not allowed to say," she said.

"*You* don't know," Jim accused her.

Marianne locked eyes with Maddy, who chewed on the inside of her cheek.

"She *might* have worked it out," Maddy admitted.

"How?" Jim demanded. But Marianne had already gone back to her book. He snorted and turned back to the table. "Are we going to play or not?"

"Would you like to play, dear?" Maddy asked me.

"No, I'm going to try to figure out where that door is," I said, lying.

Nick got up from the table, stretching. "Anyone need anything?"

"Are you sure the three of you don't want to play?" Sally asked. "If there's not another board, you can keep track on paper. Or two of you."

I said, "No worries, Sally. I really am too stressed out. Unless you're really just trying to get me to play so you can kick my butt."

She smiled thinly. She was anxious about *something*, and I didn't think it was me. As a matter of fact, while the first game had felt relatively friendly, it felt as though the tension had gone up as the players rearranged themselves.

The end of the table near the kitchen now held Maddy and Tony playing Bob and Austin; the other end, near the living room, held Wendy and Jim facing off against Sally and Egan.

I wasn't surprised to see the table with Wendy, Jim, and Sally settle into a tense, tight-lipped silence. Wendy was everyone else's primary suspect for the burglaries, with Sally—or someone *working* for Sally—as a runner-up. And Jim was already irritated for a couple of reasons. He was the kind of guy who would be lashing out at someone soon: either someone at the party, Marianne, or both.

But I found it odd that the other table seemed tense, too. Tony and Austin traded a lot of looks with each other, and studiously avoided looking at either Bob or Maddy. Maddy seemed oblivious—but she'd said that she'd suspected someone all along, hadn't she? Only that she wasn't sure about it. Or had she said she wasn't sure, but suspected several people? Now I couldn't remember. At any rate, she was playing close to the vest.

Bob seemed to shrink inside himself. As if he were chilled. He cleared his throat, reached for the deck of cards to deal, then hesitated.

"Did you need something, Bob?" I asked.

He froze, then looked toward me, a wide-eyed expression on his face. He looked *strange*, and he had dark circles under his eyes.

"No," he said, or at least shaped his lips that way. Not much sound came out. He looked down at the table, grabbed the deck of cards, and cleared his throat again. "Uh, no."

"You don't want a new deck of cards or anything?" I got up and opened drawers until I found the one where Maddy had pulled out the wrapped decks of cards; there was a carton like a cigarette carton in the drawer, half-full of new decks.

"No," he said. "I mean, yes."

I pulled out two new decks of cards and tossed them to Austin, who was sitting closest to me. He handed one to Bob, then slid the other one down the table to Egan.

"If you can't spot the sucker in the first half hour at the table, then you *are* the sucker," Tony said.

"Matt Damon in *Rounders*," Bob said.

Maddy counted on her fingers. "Nineteen words long, too."

Tony exploded in a messy snort of laughter that made him spill most of his can of Mountain Dew into his lap. I tossed him a towel.

Sally clucked her tongue. "You're all wet. Why don't you go change your pants?"

"No free basement door reveals," Maddy said. "You're just going to have to sit in it, Tony."

"I'm fine," Tony said, and sat on the towel. Nick brought him a cold can of soda.

With the instinct of a cat homing in on the one person in the room who hates cats, I said, "Bob, you know I'm a writer, right?"

His elbows slid a little wider on the kitchen table and he hunched into his cards. He had already tossed a card into the crib and was waiting for Maddy to throw in her last card and cut the deck. "Yeah. I haven't read any of your books, though. I just read sci fi and fantasy."

"No worries. I just wanted to explain why I was going to be so nosy. Tell me about your job. You work for a security company?"

He straightened up a little, then sighed and slumped back down again. "Yeah. Ridgeline Security Services. The same company that provides the security systems that were completely bypassed by the burglars. Pffft."

"I realize this is a somewhat sensitive subject," I continued, "but this is absolutely the kind of detail that I crave when I'm writing my books."

Maddy flashed me a grin.

Bob was hunkered over his cards and didn't notice. "Oh. You want to know so you can write about it."

"You can't be accurate with everything in fiction, but it's always better if you at least know what you're being inaccurate about," I said. "How did the burglars bypass the security system? Did they cut the wires? Did they get the security codes somehow and type them in? Were you even in town at the time?"

"No," Bob said, miserably. "I had gone out to Minneapolis to work on a project as a consultant for another firm. I didn't find out about it until I came back, either the burglary at my house or the others. I just got back yesterday."

"How did the police find out you'd been burgled on June fourth?" I asked.

Bob put his hand over his face and mumbled something.

"Sorry?" I asked

"The records on the security system," Bob said. "Uh, we read the log reports. Normal log reports have a bunch of junk in them. The ones after the house had been burgled had been wiped clean. We think they hacked into our servers at the office."

"Where's your office?"

"In Evergreen," he said. "You don't use Ridgeline for your house security, do you?"

It was a question, but he hadn't intonated it like one. It sounded as though he had already known.

"Ah, no," I said, hoping that the subject didn't dive any deeper into the fact that I didn't use a security service in the first place.

"Well, it's a good thing that you're not. Because we're having to hustle to try to fix the security flaw that allowed this to happen."

"What security..." I trailed off and raised a hand. "Sorry, I'm asking for proprietary information."

Bob barked a laugh. "The fact is, I haven't figured it out yet. We have multiple people working on it, both locally and remotely. Is it a Trojan? A virus? What? As far as I can tell, something got onto the system, sent a signal that turned off the houses' security systems on specific dates, then removed every trace of itself, so we have no idea what did it."

"You hear that thing in movies all the time," I said, "but in real life, you get about an hour's worth of explanation, and even then you don't understand it because you don't have the background."

Bob looked ill.

I added, "It's like Arthur C. Clarke said, 'Any sufficiently advanced technology is indistinguishable from magic.' When a computer professional says, 'We were attacked mysteriously, without a trace,' I always just assume they've realized that I won't understand the real explanation and are saving themselves time."

Bob laughed, relaxing a little. "I...I've never thought of that. I'm always trying to explain it. 'It was mysterious, and I'm not sure what happened. But I fixed it.' I think that's going to be my go-to from now on."

"If you ever need to know how to lie, ask a writer," I said.

Bob stiffened up again, looking more morose than before.

"Hah!" Sally said, turning around in her seat. "You, a liar? You are one of the most naïve people I've ever met."

"Oh?" I said.

"You are completely ignorant of half of what's going on around you, and you ignore the rest. You live off in your own little world." With her free hand, Sally made a dismissive gesture. "Making your castles in the air."

"You're probably right," I said.

Sounding offended, Austin said, "You can choose not to pay attention to gossip and not actually be naïve."

"That's naïve," Sally announced.

Austin rolled his eyes. "You can't just say something is naïve and expect that to be your entire argument. How do you know I'm not a serial killer?"

"Because you don't have serial killer eyes," Sally said. Then she added, "I knew a serial killer when I was younger."

"Bullshit," Austin said.

I'd heard this story before; Sally had sold a vacation cabin in the mountains to a guy who thought that he was more isolated than he really was. Maybe some mountains have some privacy, but ours often felt worse than living in a small town: everyone knew everyone else's business, usually because Sally told them.

In fact, Sally was the one who worked out what the guy was doing and turned him in to the cops. There was a SWAT team and everything. Jack and I had been in Denver when it all went down—we'd missed everything. I had run into the guy a few times at a grocery store in Evergreen. A young white guy, balding out of a widow's peak, heavy eyebrows, eyes that looked straight through you. The lights were on but there was nobody home behind them. The impression was creepy but nothing unusual—mostly because there are a lot of creepy people with flat eyes walking around these days.

Instead of listening to the story yet again, I got up, stretched, and announced that I had to pee. Nobody seemed to notice.

After using the toilet, I went into the guest room and looked around, my arms crossed over my chest.

A few moments later, Nick followed me into the room. "Figure it out?"

"Nick," I said, "*why* is Jack's longhorn skull here?"

He shrugged.

I got the impression that if I wanted the right to question him, I was going to have to answer his question—about the door to the secret basement, I presumed—without waffling. The fact that he'd asked at all told me that I was close.

Warmer...warmer...

There were two problems in finding the door to the secret basement.

First, *was* there a door? Was this all some kind of conspiracy to pull people's legs? A trick that I wouldn't put past Maddy, not at all.

But Marianne's assertion that she knew where the door was found, though, lent credence to the idea that there was such a door. She wasn't the kind of person to lie. The real reason she was sitting in the living room, reading a book, was that she couldn't keep enough lies straight—both her own and the rest of the others—to play cards with us.

That led to the second problem. Where *was* the door?

Not in the bathroom. Impractical. Too many pipes to work around.

Not against the outer walls of the house. The window wells weren't deep enough to conceal a false wall, and I'd walked around the outside of the house often enough to know there weren't any suspicious protuberances along the outside wall.

Through the floor?

The beige carpet wasn't the soft, fluffy, and difficult to maintain type found in most houses, but an industrial-style carpet. It was made of large "tiles" of carpet and could be pulled off the floor in sections easily. A carpet square could conceal an entrance in the floor—but what would conceal the fact that one of the squares of carpet was being moved on a regular basis?

Why, that large Native blanket on the floor, of course.

But it wasn't wrinkled, and the opposite corners were pinned down by the two beds: one bed against the wall by the closet, and the other bed under a window on the opposite side of the room.

The logical place was within the closet that butted up against the bathroom. The closet wasn't quite a walk-in, but was double-wide and had only a single head-height shelf with a closet rod underneath. It would be worth checking inside the closet.

However, I wanted to impress Nick with my reasoning skills. Maybe I'd even impress him enough to tell me about why Jack's longhorn skull was under that printed sheet.

So. If not the floor, then...

I let my eyes unfocus and let my gaze slide over the walls.

Now that I was looking for something, I quickly spotted a gap between panels that was wider than the others. On that panel hung the three rattan goat heads.

"Well?" Nick asked.

"I *know* Maddy didn't come up with the secret basement, and that it was here when she bought the house," I said. Something tickled the back of my head, but I pushed it aside for the moment. "But seriously? This is just like her."

I lifted the goat head closest to the crack between panels, revealing...a blank piece of wall and a small finishing nail.

Not a single secret-door catch in sight.

I had just made a complete ass of myself.

"Other one," Nick said, walking forward and lifting the goat head on the far side of the one I'd chosen—revealing a simple round doorknob with painted brown hardware. Nick mimed turning the knob and lifted a finger to his lips. *Not now.*

I nodded, and he rehung the goat head back on its place on the wall.

"But Nick...the skull...how did it..."

He put his finger back to his lips and walked out of the room.

DOWNSIZING

When I lost Jack, something terrible happened to me. I had to change my mind. It was such a massive shift that it was hard for me to match up the person I was with the person who I had been. Before...after. Two different Lizzes, two different selves.

The real reason I was struggling to write wasn't that I was no longer a writer (thank God! I don't know what I would have done), but that I wasn't the *same* writer. The plot I had in mind for the book I had been working on no longer made sense.

While I was at the conference I had just left, I had decided that I had to tell my agent and editor that: that I was no longer interested in writing the same book.

I could throw out that book and start over with the same starting conditions, but it wouldn't be the same book. Or I could keep writing from the point that I had left off—but not follow the outline that I had given to my editor.

The old Liz was gone. Reprogrammed, if you like, or erased. The old neuron pathways that had been in my brain now no longer worked: there was no input called *Jack* in reality, just his memory—and if there was no *Jack* to be had, then all my thoughts had to be rewired around him. When people say "a part of me died with him," now, I believe it. The description doesn't feel quite right for me, but it's close.

Even now, I'm perfectly aware of the fact that I haven't finished grieving—or rewiring—or whatever it is you have to do when you let go of someone who has died. There's a seal over the worst parts of the grief, the parts left to come.

"Who am I now?"

"Am I still a good person?"

"Am I ever going to come out of this darkness?"

"Why do I still keep having nightmares about killing Jack's killer, when it was just an accident?"

"If I let myself fully feel what I feel, will I wish I were dead?"

I'd felt the call of the void a few times since Jack's death. The sudden urge to take a sharp turn off the side of a mountain—but who would take care of the mess for me if I were gone? Who would be responsible? I had family, but I wasn't close to them, either literally or figuratively. I didn't hate any of them, but we didn't seem to have a lot in common: they were a group of tight-knit Midwesterners. The less said about Jack's family the better. They were assholes, and didn't even pretend to be nice about it.

Seeing the patterned sheet over the skull in Maddy's spare bedroom was doing something awful to my chest. It felt like trying to stretch a muscle when you were used to being in one certain position and no other, a muscle that had seized up for a year.

I wanted, in fact, to burst into tears.

"How *dare* you?" I asked the sheet in a vicious whisper. "How dare you?"

I wasn't sure who I was asking, or what the outrage was. I only knew that I wanted to put my hands around someone's neck and dig in. Whose? No idea.

I let myself wallow in the emotion—rage, grief, a craving for violence against existence itself—for a few moments, then went back into the bathroom and washed my face. My purse was in the other room, so I opened the medicine cabinet to grab a couple of ibuprofen, and washed them down with a handful of cold water from the sink.

I dried my face and looked in the mirror.

I looked old and stiff and forbidding, like a skeletal version of myself. A real Mrs. Danvers type: disapproving and almost lunatic. I barely recognized myself. I wondered if I would ever recover a feeling of security and happiness. How could I? My security and happiness was on the other side of the mirror, and me with no way to bring him back.

I shook my head.

I had to stay focused on the present. I had to tell myself that what was going on was a natural and normal part of grief. My brain was rewiring itself, and it was exhausted. When your brain is too tired, it starts to turn on itself. I was really just upset that I couldn't have what I wanted. I was being a child...

Telling myself those things didn't help.

Or rather they didn't make me feel *better*. But they at least made me aware that my feeling bad wasn't strange or unusual or out of place. Which was an improvement.

But the fact was that, even a year later, I still kept cycling around Jack's death like a moth to a flame.

Why did you die? Why did you die? Why did you die?

How dare you?

———

By the time I finally got control of myself and returned to the kitchen-slash-living room, it was obvious that I had been crying. Which was for the best. Look like you've been crying, and people won't ask you where you've been for the last twenty minutes.

The conversation had turned again. Now Jim was talking about how he and Marianne were talking about downsizing from their current residence to somewhere smaller.

"Not because it would be *cheaper*," Jim said. "Oh, no. The place Marianne has me looking at isn't *cheap*. It's like a cruise ship, only it's a retirement community."

"You're not old enough for a retirement community," Sally said.

I blinked. The thing that had been tickling in the back of my head in the guest room now came to the front: *Sally had sold this house to Maddy*. That meant Sally knew about the basement already, and presumably knew how to get into the basement.

Didn't it? Didn't things like that have to be disclosed to your realtor when you built the house?

The house wasn't that old. The secret basement would have had to be on the appraisal...would it have to be listed on real estate websites, I wondered? Probably not the latter.

Sally knew everything and everybody. She had probably known about the secret basement when the house had been built in the first place.

The flash of insight didn't take more than a second or two. Jim said, in a proud tone, "We have to think ahead. I don't want to cling to the past to the point where I end up falling down some stairs with a broken hip."

Sitting down at a stool at the kitchen island, I said, "What does Marianne think about it?"

It was a troublesome question, given that Marianne was sitting in the living room next to us.

"Marianne thinks it's a good idea," Jim said without hesitation.

"What will you do with all your stuff?" I asked. Jim had an enormous garage full of bikes; I'd had to stand around, drinking too many beers, while he showed Jack around when we first moved in. I couldn't imagine that he'd sold any off since then.

"We'll each keep one or two," Jim said. "The place we have in mind has its own garage. It works on a system where you start out in a townhouse, then move into an assisted living apartment, then into a nursing room. We'll get rid of the bikes when we're ready to move into less spacious quarters."

Marianne said, "I'm the one who's obsessed with them, you know."

It came out of the blue. Even Jim wasn't expecting it: his face turned red. But he said, "I met her on a motocross racetrack."

Marianne said, "I love the feeling of flying. But I'm terrified of heights. I have to take a sedative every time we fly. Being on the open road is my true...calling. I like motocross well enough, but not as much as Jim does. He loves the competition."

It almost felt like she had been about to say *true love* and had only stopped herself just in time.

"She's a superb racer in the women's class," Jim said.

Oh boy.

"Jim was in the special forces and I was doing a technical job at a military base," she said. "There was a track nearby and we hit it off. He bought me a drink, a cosmopolitan." She laughed. "Not my drink. But we've been together almost fifteen years now, both of us divorced from our first marriages. And still riding."

She sounded surprised, as if she were shocked to be where she was at the moment. I wondered where it was she had planned to be instead. How old were they? Younger than Maddy, younger than Sally but not by much. Late sixties? I wasn't sure. But surely that couldn't be right. If they were in their late sixties and had been married for fifteen years, they would have been fifty or so when they met. Special forces guys don't stay in the special forces until they're fifty. They get promoted, injured, retire out. Jim had been a sergeant at Fort Carson, Colorado, before he retired; Marianne had worked at a nearby Air Force base as a contractor. That much I knew.

And I didn't know much about motocross, but I knew that it was physically demanding, far more than trail or road riding. It seemed odd that they were still riding in races—even exhibition races.

As if reading my mind, Jim said, "We really should have retired a long time ago. Made way for the younger generations. I'm not getting any younger."

Marianne said, "It was nice to ride with you, Jim, in Vegas."

For some reason, this set him back for a second. "It was, wasn't it?" he said, without any real emotion.

She smiled, looked out the window for a few moments to watch the rain hitting the windowpanes. I, personally, was starting to wonder if it was going to hail. Lightning flashed nearby, and the nearly-immediate thunder made the house shiver.

"We should be thinking about who's going to have to stay the night!" Sally said.

"I'll take a look at the driveway," Nick said, and excused himself toward the back of the house, where the back door led from the laundry room to the garage.

"I'll be fine," I said.

"We will, too," Jim said.

Marianne said, "As long as Liz will give us a ride back home."

"That's right," Jim said.

"No problem," I said.

The games were put on hold out of respect for Nick—and because neither Wendy nor I wanted to sit in for him.

"What day was the race?" I asked.

"June sixth," Marianne said.

"I'll have to look it up and see if they took photos of you."

"They got plenty of Marianne," Jim said. "She's the pretty one."

We all laughed politely, even though it was only mildly funny.

I thought *June sixth was the day that Wendy cleaned my house.* Jim and Marianne's house had been burgled on May thirty-first. They hadn't come home until after the house had been burgled, but they knew it had been on May thirty-first.

"How did you find out your house had been burgled?" I asked.

Marianne said, "The police called us on the fifth. Jim wanted to go home, but I insisted we stay for another day and finish out the race."

Sally said, "I should have noticed earlier that something was off. You know how I like to keep an eye on all of you. But I didn't notice until the fifth, when I called the police."

"What did you notice?" I asked.

"You can't see much from the road," Marianne said. "But I had a feeling, nonetheless. I called the police to have them check up on the house. I don't like to drive up anyone's driveways when they're not home, of course. But I had a feeling. When the police came to the house, they could see in through the window that things had been disturbed."

"In through the window?" I asked.

"Yes, the drapes on the front window were open," Sally said, nodding. "All anyone had to do was drive up the driveway and look right in."

"And could they tell how the burglars broke in?"

"They were professionals," Sally said. "They must have used a lockpick on the front door! That's what the police said."

"They said a lockpick had definitely been used?" I asked.

"No, well, I was waiting for them near the house and I overheard one of them talking to the other," Sally admitted. "All they said was that they *must* have used a lockpick." She looked at me suspiciously, then at Wendy, who was standing in the kitchen, listening but not really doing much else. "What else could they have used?"

"A key," said Jim. "There are quite a few people who have each other's keys around here. Wendy has 'em, doesn't she? So she can clean."

"So does Sally," I said dryly. "Unless you've changed the locks since she showed your house."

"I keep keys for all the houses I've sold," Sally announced. "Not that it would do me much good if I wanted to break into your house or anyone else's, with the security systems you have.

And I can't imagine that Wendy would be able to manage it, either. Neither one of *us* has any technical background."

"Bob does," Jim said.

"So do you," Marianne said. "Don't you, Jim? From work."

"That was years ago," Jim said. "Security systems have moved on since then, and I was never an expert in home security systems. Only the IT work."

"IT security *is* home security," Bob said. "Because of the way that ours report back to the servers at the office."

Maddy said, "I don't understand why on earth you would rely on a wireless signal to carry messages from a home security system to your office. Everyone knows how unreliable those are."

Bob said, "We use phone lines. There's a separate jack installed."

"Oh, so every time someone calls the house, you lose your security system!" Maddy announced. "Just like when everyone used to use modems on the phone lines."

"No, we can run them both at the same time by..." Bob looked at me helplessly. "Uh, I mean, we worked out a solution where a phone call doesn't boot your security system off the network."

"Magic," Maddy said bitterly.

I laughed. Bob had just tried out my explanation trick on Maddy.

Austin said, "So here's the score as I see it. Everyone suspects everyone else. The people who have all the keys don't have the technical know-how to kill the security systems. The people who have the technical know-how don't have the physical keys. The people with the technical know-how weren't here when the burglaries were happening. Wendy and Sally were here, either cleaning houses or snooping around. Maddy hasn't been burgled, but she's sticking her nose in anyway. And then there's Liz, the writer, who doesn't fit in either as a person with keys or a person with technical know-how. Why did she get burgled? And Wendy has keys, but instead of getting robbed, her house got smooshed. What's up with that? Do we need to start asking who has chainsaws?"

We all had chainsaws. This wasn't surprising, though, given that we lived up in the mountains, where the important question wasn't "did the tree make a sound if there was no one there to hear it" but "how am I going to get up my damned driveway?"

I sucked on my lips. I had been asking myself the same questions. Plus one more. "You forgot the important part, Austin," I said. "Who benefits?"

Austin, sitting in his place at the table, raised both hands flat out and said, "Whoa, whoa, whoa. Let's not get complicated, here. They don't address motive in Clue. Who did it with what weapon in what room. That's all you need to know in order to solve a mystery."

Everyone but me laughed.

Maddy said, "Well, if you had *told* me that you wanted to play *Clue*, I would have found the box where I left it when I moved in."

"In the basement?" I asked hopefully, and everyone laughed.

"So you haven't figured out where the secret door is yet?" Austin said.

I shook my head sadly. "I thought I had, but no."

It's not technically lying, after all, if you're playing a game and you're holding a card that says, *You must not reveal the location of the secret door to the basement.* It's just following the rules on the card.

Playing the game.

Austin winked at me. I frowned at him, looking puzzled.

You must not reveal the location of the secret door to the basement was a serious card. You didn't just wink back when it might give the location of the basement away. What if someone reasoned out that I'd been looking in or around the guest room?

Now Austin looked toward Nick, asking the unaskable question.

Nick said, "Need something, Austin?"

"I guess not," Austin said disgustedly.

Then a flash of lightning so bright that it was blinding even through the windows hit us.

I rubbed my eyes, seeing spots.

"Damn it!" Jim said, his voice almost drowned out by the immediate roll of thunder.

I opened my eyes. The lights had gone out. The room was perfectly pitch black, with not even the faintest glow from outside. At least, until another flash of lightning split the sky.

After a moment, from the living room came a soft, white light, oblong in shape: Marianne had pulled out her phone and was aiming it toward us. Within moments, several of us had taken out our phones and were using them to shine in each others' faces, uselessly. Jim told everyone that they should take turns using phones rather than everyone wiping out their batteries all at once. Bob said that he had about a dozen phone chargers outside in his car. Austin, acting like a smartass, wanted to know if everyone should start prepping for the zombie apocalypse or what. Tony argued that a zombie apocalypse was unlikely and we should really be prepping for Chinese hackers to take down our energy infrastructure. Jim angrily demanded to know where Tony was getting the idea that the Chinese were trying to shoot lightning at us all, anyway. Austin said that nobody said the Chinese were shooting lightning at anyone.

Marianne said, in a strained voice, "He's just hoping to start an argument. Jim, this isn't one of your online bulletin boards.

It's not the liberals' fault that the power went out, so don't even go there."

Maddy sent Nick and Egan outside with a couple of super-bright LED flashlights to check around the house for fire and downed power lines. They came back completely soaked and with the report that they couldn't see evidence of any power lines being down—but that the road was flooded out.

"Is it washed out?" Maddy asked worriedly.

Not as far as they could tell, but who could tell if the flooding kept up. Maddy announced that everyone should plan to stay for the night, or at least until the water had gone down.

I mentally counted heads: the only two people in the house who didn't know where the secret door was were Bob and Jim. I hadn't seen any real evidence that Wendy knew, but who else was going to clean the basement? Maddy seemed to trust Wendy implicitly.

Wendy was bringing out flashlights, candles, and oil lamps from various nooks and crannies, providing more weight to the idea that she knew the location of everything in the house.

"So if we're going to stay the night, we're going to find out where the secret door is," Bob said, a question rising in his voice.

"That's right," Jim said.

"Not necessarily," said Maddy. "It depends on how observant you are."

"I'm pretty observant," Jim said.

"Are you?" Maddy said. "You didn't find it before this."

"That's not fair!" Jim exclaimed. "I didn't even know the basement existed."

"A good detective doesn't need to know that a crime happened in order to become aware of its existence," Maddy said.

"Oh, so you're saying that you knew about the burglaries before anyone else did?" Jim said.

"Might have done," Maddy said. "I *might* have known about the burglaries even before Sally did, and she discovered one of them."

Jim snorted. "The only way you could have done that was by doing the burglaries yourself."

Maddy held up her hands, which, even in the candle- and lamplight, were old and more than a bit wrinkly. "With these hands?" she asked. "And my hip? But you forget the possibility that I saw certain patterns happening which could only lead to burglaries which then occurred."

"You're no Miss Marple," said Jim.

"I will have you know," said Maddy, with great dignity, "that I won a prize in elementary school for solving crossword puzzles."

Jim guffawed. "That has nothing to do with it!"

"Seems that way," Wendy murmured, so softly that I was probably the only one to hear her. Wendy and I had both returned to the kitchen, and were sitting on stools at the island together. Wendy glanced toward me and pressed her lips together, not so much disapprovingly, I thought, but as though she wanted to tell me of something but had decided against it.

I wondered if Maddy had forbidden her from telling me something, another card in the game Maddy was playing...

Maddy cleared her throat. "So. You're all probably wondering why I gathered you here together tonight."

"No fair," interrupted Tony. "So many movies say that, that it's not a fair quote."

She flashed him a little smile, then a frown to tell him that his interruption was over now. "I've called you here because I've figured out who has been burglarizing your houses."

That brought everyone up short for a moment.

Then everyone seemed to be talking at once: Jim protested his innocence, Sally protested hers, Bob wanted to know how Maddy had found out, it wasn't possible without his records at the office, and Austin was saying, "Wait, so this was really all an amateur detective novel and it's time for the big reveal and I just helped by setting up the information before the lights went out? *Cooool*."

Nick crossed his arms across his chest and stared at me for a moment across the length of the kitchen table.

Something was coming.

The uproar lasted a few moments, then faded into cantankerous expectation.

When it was quiet enough for her to be heard, Maddy said, "Hear me out."

"You're nuts," Jim said. "Why should I?"

"Because you can't get out of the driveway," Maddy announced cheerfully. "Unless you think that Liz's SUV could make it?" she asked Nick and Egan.

Nick shook his head. Egan said, "I can go check it again, if you want."

Jim waved a hand toward the table and said, "It doesn't matter. I'll have to hear the old bitch out anyway, either now or via gossip. Might as well get my bullshit from the horse's mouth."

"That's a mixed-species metaphor," Maddy said. "I'll pretend you didn't say it."

"Pretend whatever you like," Jim snapped.

"So who did it?" Austin asked.

Maddy turned toward me.

In the back of my mind, I knew I'd been dragged into the middle of this mess on purpose. The burglars at *my* house had been too neat and too selective, for one thing, courteously stealing the one thing that would have dragged me out of the house on a night like this. And then arranging, via Wendy, that I should see it.

Maddy lifted her arm slowly, a la Donald Sutherland in *Invasion of the Body Snatchers*. I half expected her to start making an unnatural, alien shriek. She pointed at me.

"Liz," she said. In a perfectly normal tone of voice.

I clenched my jaw and said nothing.

Everyone looked at me; the expressions on their faces were somewhat softened by the candlelight, but were still easily read:

Jim's eyes narrowed, Bob's looked completely shocked and dismayed—as if he had already been thinking it, but was surprised that anyone else had been—and Sally rolled her eyes. Nick still had his arms crossed over his chest, Austin was one of the shocked ones, Tony nodded, and Egan glanced at me, then looked away.

Egan said, "It's still pouring and nobody's gonna be able to get home. No disrespect, but are you sure you really want to start something like this with everyone trapped in your house all night?"

Maddy cackled. "Too late to take it back now!"

I raised my hand. "May I ask a question? Why accuse me? I got burgled myself. You may have noticed. I don't have the skills to burgle someone's house. And I wasn't even here. I should be the opposite of a suspect."

"Oh, Liz," Maddy said deprecatingly. "You're not as naïve as people believe. Don't try to think you can play that card *now*. Pay attention."

"Just asking," I said peevishly. My heart was pounding and my palms sweating. I wished that Maddy had given me some kind of warning beforehand. Except she had, hadn't she? When she'd asked me to come over in the first place.

"First," Maddy said, "you write mysteries. Moreover, you write *clever* mysteries. That means you have the kind of convoluted mind that could come up with such a plot. And you've researched all sorts of things that nobody else would bother with. Who's to say that you don't know how to pick locks?"

I didn't respond. As a matter of fact, I *did* know how to pick locks...badly. As in, I could pick a translucent practice lock in about seven minutes, and regular locks not at all. But I *had* lock picks, and I *had* experience with lockpicking, and my browser history was speckled with hits for YouTube lockpicking videos that I had watched obsessively over the last few months, as I researched for my fantasy of avenging Jack's death. Picking locks was the least of what I'd researched.

If anyone checked my computer, I was screwed.

"Another point," Maddy said. "In one of Liz's recent books, there's a scene where two amateurs break into someone's house and bypass the security system by having an accomplice take down the security firm monitoring the system."

"They used a different method in the book," I protested. "The accomplice hacked into the system, but they just introduced a virus that corrupted the computers monitoring the alarms."

Maddy raised her eyebrows and looked significantly around the room, as if I were surrounded by a jury of my peers instead of sitting in a kangaroo court. I was starting to get really irritated.

"As for her claim that she wasn't in Colorado at the time of the burglaries, how do we know that? She claims to have been at a writer's conference in—where was it?"

"Minneapolis," I said, suddenly remembering that Bob had said that he had been in Minneapolis, too.

"It's easy enough to drive away from one's house, pretend to fly off to another state, switch cars, wear a pair of sunglasses, and return to the neighborhood," Maddy said.

Well. I pursed my lips. *That* brought some interesting ideas to mind. For example, who *else* might have claimed to be out of town, but really wasn't?

"All of this is interesting, but it just suggests that I *might* have been able to do it," I said. "However inconvenient it is to your theory, Maddy, any of us can google me on the Internet and find about a hundred pictures of me with fans at the dates and times I was actually there, though."

A couple of phones came out. Austin's was one of them.

"Ugh," he said. "Signal's down."

"How *inconvenient*," Maddy said. "We can't check the veracity of your story, Liz, at the exact moment that it needs to be checked."

"Are you trying to accuse me of doing something to take our cell phones down?" I demanded. I pulled my cell phone off the counter and checked the signal: completely dead. "And, sorry, but what the hell even kind of motivation would I have had to rob *houses*? I'm not exactly broke, you know."

Maddy shook her head in the dim glow of the candle- and cell-phone light. She took a breath, then let it go, her narrow, pinched shoulders sagging and her head falling forward, as if she were gathering strength.

Nick said, "You okay, Maddy?"

Maddy straightened up. "No, no. I'm not all right. You'll have to excuse me a moment." She stood up from her chair at the table, and, putting her hand on the shoulders of her guests as she walked past them, made her way into the kitchen, where she circled around Wendy, then stopped at the sink, taking a glass from one of the cupboards above the sink. She reached into a pocket and pulled out something small that she downed quickly and chased with cold water from the sink. A pill?

I stared at her, helpless to move or really even breathe.

"What *is* this all about, Maddy?" I asked. It all seemed too improbable to be true, either the idea that I had stolen something or—as I was sure other people at the party had begun to suspect—that Maddy was losing her marbles.

Maddy only shook her head. "I need to lie down, dear," she said.

Wendy said, "Should I—send one of the boys out to get some help?"

"No, no," Maddy said. "I'm just wondering what kind of fool I've been this last month, that's all. If you'll excuse me, I need to lie down and think about what I've done. Forget about my accusing you, dear, that was all wrong. I see it now. Completely the wrong approach."

And then she walked—no, hobbled—down the hallway toward her room, bearing neither candle nor cell phone to light the way. Softly, a door closed.

I looked around the table of people, who were all staring at me as though I had all the answers.

"So what does the great mystery writer have to say for herself?" snarled Jim.

I said, "I got nothing."

The Nothing

The power was still out and there was still no signal on anyone's cell phone. Jim declared that he was going to get home if he had to wade through floodwaters to do it.

"You'd go rolling down the mountain if you tried it," Marianne said. She'd gone back to reading a book, but now it was on her phone.

More to keep the peace than anything else, I said, "Let's go outside and check on the state of the road."

I put my jacket and shoes on with my purse strap underneath my jacket, so it would take a little longer for my purse to get wet in the still-ongoing downpour. We couldn't see much by candlelight, which just reflected our own faces back to us, but every time the lightning flashed, we could see the windows on the sides of the house sheeting with water. It seemed to be coming from every direction. Leaves and pine needles were plastered to the glass, and outside there was a vague sense of violent movement.

Thunder roared, rain rattled, and every once in a while, we all looked up to the ceiling, squinting at it, at the sudden rise in volume as a sudden burst of hail hit the roof.

Jim and I walked toward the back door by the utility room; he wanted to check on his bike before we left. I was fine with that; my SUV was sort of in the same direction. Nick came up behind us with heart-stopping suddenness and said, "Take a flashlight."

I took one and clicked it on. Jim ignored him and opened the door to a curtain of water running out of the gutters on the roof overhang. A ridge of white hail lay on the cement pad in front of the door.

"Shit," Jim said. "It really is coming down. I was starting to think that it was all faked."

I snorted; the sound was covered by the crash of bouncing balls of ice. I dug out my keys and hit the unlock button until I saw a flash of headlights. "There's the SUV," I said.

Jim looked back and forth, as if expecting a train to come barreling between house and garage any moment, then ran across to the side door of the garage without another word, leaving a Jim-sized hole in the curtain of water and ice as he went.

I shone a light over the gravel between the house and where I had parked, looking to see if anything had been knocked down into my path. I didn't want to trip and fall on a tree branch. But it looked clear. I took a deep breath.

"Nick," I said, without turning around, "Did you break into my house and steal that skull of Jack's?"

"Yeah," he said.

"Why?"

"To be sure that you came tonight. But you knew that."

"But why did you do it? And how did you even get it here, on those bikes?"

No answer.

I went running out into the storm.

———

I got in the SUV and started it, then slowly backed up until I was able to turn around. Fortunately there weren't that many cars—just my SUV, Bob's SUV (a very similar, dark model), Wendy's old, peeling Toyota, and Sally's flashy Cadillac. Maddy's Lincoln Continental had been sold some time ago; she didn't have a driver's license any more. Otherwise, just the Griffiths' and the boys' bikes, which were all in the garage, although I couldn't see them now—the garage door had been lowered, probably before the boys had come back into the house after I had arrived.

I backed carefully between the house and the garage and waited for Jim to come back out of the garage. After a couple of minutes, I honked the horn. A few seconds later, there was a bang as the garage side door whipped inward—presumably banging into the wall—and Jim stepped out.

His face was so angry-looking that I almost hit the lock button on the door. But then I thought about him taking that mood back inside the house and using it like a whip on someone else, and carefully schooled a blank look onto my face instead.

He threw open my passenger door and stood on the ground, getting even wetter. "What now?"

"I'm ready to drive out to check the road. Coming or not?"

"I don't trust anyone but my own two eyes at this point." He climbed in and slammed the door behind him.

I rolled my eyes and put the SUV into gear, then crept forward with the headlights on low. Putting on high beams in rain that heavy is like putting on your high beams in fog or a blizzard. All you do is blind yourself.

The drive wasn't that steep, as far as gravel drives in the mountains went, but it wasn't *flat*, either. The first section was okay, except for the split-rail fence on one side that led down the side of the mountain. Then there was a sharp turn, this time with no fence to tell you where the road left off and the mountain started—and a big boulder protruding on the other side, narrowing the roadway.

Right after the boulder, the road suddenly dropped into a steep downgrade for a few hundred yards. Then it came out of the trees and onto a meadow, crossing a stream as it did so, using a cement culvert. Hypothetically, the water would run through the culvert and not over the road. However, the creek tended to collect the runoff of half a mountain's worth of water.

Both sides of the road on either side of the stream were wider than the rest of the road, specifically so cars could turn around, which told you how often the creek flooded out the road. As in, every single spring and a couple of times every summer, during big storms like this one.

Slowly, with great caution and even cowardice, I rolled to the first turn in the road, making sure not to hit the boulder, but not daring to get too far away from it, either. It was a case of Scylla and Charybdis, with my SUV navigating the narrow passage between two dangers and hoping that I wouldn't feel a sudden lurch as a tire slid off the gravel. *This* part of the road might have washed out, too.

But the SUV stayed stable.

The road seemed to drop out of view in front of us, the headlights only brightening the rain and hail in front of us. The hail wasn't too bad at that point; the trees directly around the house had been cleared away as a firebreak, but the road was surrounded by them, and the heavy pines blocked the worst of the bouncing hail, even if I *was* unreasonably convinced that every crack meant that the front windshield would shatter and fall in on us.

The downhill stretch was mostly straight, but I still had to focus to make sure there wasn't anything in front of us. Lots of smaller tree branches were already down, and scraped against the bottom of the SUV.

"If I had known this was going to take a goddamned hour--!" Jim said at one point.

I ignored him, reminding myself that I was doing this to keep him out of Maddy's hair.

We made it to the next turn, where the creek and road met and crossed each other. I pulled up to a stop in front of what looked like a blank wall of water in front of us, then put the SUV in park and smashed the parking brake to the floor.

"Christ!" Jim exclaimed. "Look at that!"

I opened the door and got out. There are some things you do as a writer just so you can have experienced them, and therefore write about them. It was raining so hard that I literally couldn't see past the edge of the creek, which was definitely flooding the road.

"What the hell?" Jim yelled. He also got out.

I pulled my jacket closed. I was already shivering with the cold. The hail was only pea-sized—mostly. The water completely covered the road ahead of us. Not just the part where the creek crossed with the road, but the entire drive as it turned sharply to the left on the other side, where it disappeared behind a stand of aspens.

Past the drive, it was like looking at the end of the world. Just...nothing.

I grew up in a couple of different upper plains states, so I'm not unfamiliar with the experience of looking out into the weather and seeing what looks like a perfectly solid wall during a blizzard. I'm not even unfamiliar with the experience of deciding that "it's not *too* bad" and driving through it. We're all teenagers at some point, after all.

What shook me about this one was the sense that the world in front of me wasn't just blocked off by a wall of water, but erased. I think that it was the pure *sound* of it that did it. The sound wasn't just wind or rain or thunder (although it contained all of those things), but a belly-deep rumble that my subconscious decided was the sound of reality falling apart, like in *The Neverending Story* when the Nothing starts destroying whatever land it was the characters were in.

What was left was only what we had with us: cell phones that didn't work, power that had been cut off, a single house, and a number of guests who, if they weren't ready to start killing each other, would be soon.

Who would be the first to die, I wondered, then felt my throat tighten.

Maddy.

———

Somehow I made it back to the SUV, closing the door behind me. Again, I was tempted to lock the door and leave Jim behind. It wasn't anything he did or said. The look on his face in the reflected lo-beams of the SUV wasn't angry anymore, but filled with a kind of awe at the storm. *Finally*, I remember thinking, *he's faced something with more bluster than he has. It must be like seeing the face of your own personal god or something.*

I'm not sure what exactly I was thinking. Maybe I just wanted to get back to Maddy without any stupid delays. Maybe I just wanted to protect her from what I thought would be Jim's inevitable outburst at finding out that he couldn't have what he wanted—that was, to get out of here as soon as possible.

Either way, I had to force myself to keep my hands on the steering wheel instead of locking the door, gripping so hard that one of my knuckles popped.

He threw open the door and got in. "Whew! That's some storm. Good luck getting turned around."

I took a deep breath and shook my head. I *would* have to turn around, wouldn't I? I somehow hadn't thought that far ahead.

I turned around slowly, wincing every time I felt the tug of the rushing waters on the front or back end of the tires. I managed to make it a five-point turn somehow, and aimed the SUV back up the road, making it about halfway up the steep section of road before a heavy downfall of hail made me stop in the middle of the road, then put the SUV into park.

"What are you doing?"

"I can't see," I said shortly. I had had just about enough of Jim's presence.

"Why did you break into my house?" he asked abruptly.

"I didn't."

"Don't lie to me," he snapped.

"It's not on me to prove that I didn't, but you to prove that I did," I said.

"But I know you did."

"Feel free to walk the rest of the way back to the house," I said. "If you're in such a hurry."

"What, do you think you're going to be able to throw me out of the car?"

"You knew Jack," I said, pointedly. "Do you think I *don't* have a handgun or mace in the side pocket of the door? Trust me. I have ways to get you out of the car if I don't want you here."

He stopped to think for a moment. "Why did you ask me to come out here with you to check the road? You didn't need to bring me. You could have done it all by yourself."

"To get you out of Maddy's hair," I said. "You're an asshole, Maddy's not feeling well, and you tend to lash out at the closest available victim."

"Are you saying I abuse my wife?" he demanded.

If I hadn't just seen him lash out at the boys, trying to force them into an argument about Chinese lightning, I might have fallen for it.

"Yes," I said, in all seriousness, even though I'd never seen a sign of it. It was one of those moments where you say something that's kind of a throwaway statement, then realize that it only popped out of your mouth because you subconsciously knew it already. A truth.

He didn't answer.

I added, "And if I were you, I'd watch your back."

"What are you saying?"

"I don't know," I said. "Why don't you jump to your own conclusions instead of shouting at me about mine?"

We *were* shouting, I realized. Every word we had said in the echoing tin can of the SUV had been necessarily in a raised tone of voice; the rain would have drowned us out otherwise. But now we were aggressively, deliberately shouting.

I took one of those deep breaths in which you try to convince yourself that counting to ten is going to do any good whatsoever. I was taunting the bear for the satisfaction of seeing it get pissed off. What did I expect was going to happen? I think I was seriously hoping for an excuse to use the bear spray in the side pocket.

"What on earth would make you think there was anything to Maddy's crazy theory, anyway?" I asked. "I mean, what the fuck could I even want of yours?"

At that point, I wasn't trying to get any kind of reaction out of him, pissed or otherwise. I just couldn't follow why he had even decided to say something like that. To get my goat? While I was driving through a thunderstorm in the mountains? I can normally at least follow people's irrational reasoning. This time I couldn't even get a hold of a single thread of it.

Jim seemed to deflate. He went quiet for so long that the hail died down enough for me to put the SUV back into gear and continue creeping back up the mountain.

"Nothing," he said, finally, as I pulled the SUV in between the house and the garage again. "I have literally nothing you could want."

After Jim got out of the SUV, I sat there by myself, shaking and angry and hurt and a hundred other things. I get that it was irrational. Even at the time, I knew it was irrational. Jim and I had snapped at each other. Jim was an asshole. The spat hadn't even ended in recriminations, just a quiet statement by Jim. He hadn't even slammed the door on the way out. So why was I so completely upset?

I cried it out while the rain and the hail came down, hoping that the door of the house wouldn't open and fill with concerned faces checking up on me. I wouldn't have been able to handle it.

"Get a grip," I said out loud, eventually. It was so loud in the SUV that I could barely hear myself.

I was shivering with cold. I wasn't wearing the kind of jacket engineered to throw off water and wick away sweat, just an old cotton field coat, the kind that my dad used to wear out to the barn in the autumn to take care of the animals we kept, growing up. I was soaked through. I turned the heat on in the SUV. I still hadn't shut off the engine. Soon the windows were covered with fog, and I was completely sealed in. I shut off the headlights and sat there in the dashboard lights, wondering if I should crawl into the back and dig out my emergency sleeping bag. I decided against it, but it did make me turn around in the seat and see my laptop bag still in the back.

Laying the bag across my lap to keep the laptop from getting wet, I booted my laptop. Of course the first thing I did was check for a wifi signal. Nada. Zilch. There was no power at the house, though, so I wasn't surprised. I did laugh at myself for being such a creature of habit.

I pulled up my latest story file and opened it.

This wasn't as easy as I just described it. It had been over a month since I had last opened the file, and for a few moments I couldn't remember which the right version was. I normally keep close track—writers have a horror of losing wordcount or sending the wrong version of a story out—but the last few times I'd actually worked on the file, I hadn't been able to bring myself to update the version number according to a system that I'd been using since my early twenties. It just didn't matter enough at the time.

I scrolled to the end of the file, fussing about the slowness of the file loading. Then the thing happened that always happens when you stop working on a story for a while: I couldn't remember what the fuck I'd been writing when I'd left off, let alone what I'd intended to write next.

The person who had written those words was gone now.

I mean, that's a melodramatic statement, right? And I could have chalked it up to the changes wrought by grief. *Grief had made me into a different person. I will never be able to write this story again.* That would have been fair, right?

Except that writers *always* feel that way. Death of a spouse or not. And listening to myself react so dramatically to just *looking* at the story made me laugh out loud.

Normal. What I was feeling was normal.

For the first time in a year.

———

When I stopped to stretch my cramped wrists (a laptop balanced between your lap and the steering wheel of an SUV isn't the most comfortable place to write), an hour had passed and I was feeling the warm glow of creativity on me for the first time in forever. It felt like the light was starting to come through the cracks, like I was starting to feel a little more myself.

I hadn't really accomplished much. All I had done, really, was back up a chapter or two and reread what I had written, while snorting at typos and one particularly stupid mistake I'd made, where the serial killer in the past—in the 1600s, if you remember—had quoted someone who I now recognized to be Thomas Paine.

As in, the Thomas Paine who hadn't even been born until seventeen thirty-something, had participated in the American

Revolutionary War, and had been imprisoned in France during the French Revolution.

Urk.

But, slowly, as I read and reviewed and processed the word-processor file in front of me, the story-processor file in my head had finally been found, reassembled (it had fragmented into a bajillion disconnected parts), and opened, and I could actually remember, more or less, what the story was supposed to be about.

I added about fifty new words, wrote down a few notes underneath about where I thought the plot might go next, and saved the file. Then I shut down the laptop, closed it, kissed my first two fingers, and laid that kiss on the lid of the laptop, for luck. I put it back into the bag and zipped it shut, carefully tucking it under the seat behind me, as the precious thing it was.

Although, honestly, the SUV could have been hit by lightning at that exact second and fried all the electronics in the car, erasing my updates forever, and I wouldn't have cared. Beginning writers think—and at times, *all* writers think—that it's all about finding the perfect draft, and that their careers will be over if something goes wrong and they lose one.

Not so. The important part is never the little black marks on the page, but something I'd lost for a while, and now, somehow, despite being falsely accused of robbing my neighbors' houses by a woman who I'd had nothing but respect for...

I had it back.

I turned off the SUV and waited for the next break between hail showers, then ran inside the back door and into the utility room. That whole time, either no one had checked on me, or else I hadn't noticed. Honestly, I was so involved in what I was reading and typing, it was probably the latter.

I stopped inside the door, stamping my feet as though I had just come in from a blizzard. It was about forty degrees outside, and I had run through about an ankle's worth of hail pebbles and slush with my breath steaming for two breaths in front of me before I made it back into the house.

The first thing I did was strip off my jacket and hang it on a rack of little wooden pegs by the door. The person who had built the house had left the pegs within easy reach of little hands, which meant the ends of my jacket dragged on the floor. I kicked off my shoes on the rubber mat and squelched into the dark hallway, leaving wet footprints on the floor behind me. Comfy, no-tie travel shoes are not the best thing ever for walking around in the rain.

The house was quiet. *Too* quiet. The living room was lit, but seemed at first glance empty. It wasn't; Marianne was still sitting in the same seat, looking at her phone. She now had a flat white external battery pack attached to it.

"Where is everyone?" I asked, then realized: they must all have gone downstairs.

To the secret basement.

Without me.

Marianne said, "Don't forget, you brought a spare bag with you and left it by the front door."

"Thanks," I said. There were dry clothes in that bag. "Are they downstairs?"

"Yes."

"And you're not?"

By the dim glow of her phone screen, I saw her grimace with one side of her face. "No."

I waited. Then I walked across the room and sat wetly in the chair beside her. "Marianne, I want to ask you something."

"Shoot," she said.

But then I didn't know what to ask. I knew I wanted to know something, but what was it? Why Jim was such a bastard? Whether she actually loved, or even liked, him? Why was she still with him? *Was* he abusive?

All that came out was: "Why...?"

Her eyes flicked up at me. I don't know what it was, but suddenly she seemed as gorgeous as an old-fashioned movie star. A *femme fatale*.

"Why what?"

She wasn't going to fill in the blanks for me.

I suddenly flashed on an incident that had happened after we first met the two of them. It had been the same day that we'd done that weird tour of their house and seen all Jim's bikes. I had retreated to the kitchen, where I'd been trying to make some kind of connection with Marianne. I remembered thinking that I had to get along with her somehow, but that it would be harder to make a connection with her than even with her asshole husband.

"Do you remember that day you invited us over to your house?" I asked. "Jack and I?"

"Vaguely," she said.

"We were standing in the kitchen trying to think of what to say to each other, at least, I was trying to think of what to say to *you*, and we both looked out the window over the sink at the same time. Jack and Jim were standing in the sunlight beside the garage and smiling at each other, and we both said, 'Oh shit, there they go again' at the same time."

"I remember," she said.

The image was kind of burned into my memory. Jack, who was slightly shorter than Jim, was standing on the balls of his feet, almost on tiptoe, with his chest thrust forward. Jim had straightened up so that his spine was an iron rod. His chin had jutted out to made his neck look distorted. The cords on both men's necks were standing out and their fists held lightly—not tightly—with the thumbs outside the fingers. And they were *smiling*.

"They looked like they were about to start a fistfight," I said.

She looked back down at her phone. "They were only smiling at each other."

"What were they arguing about? Do you know? Jack blew it off when I asked him. Then he said something about arguing about which of their bikes was better, but I didn't believe him."

"Were you in the habit of disbelieving your husband?"

It was a bland statement, at least in tone, but I leaned toward her. "Are you?"

She looked up at me, steadily, without avoidance or nervousness, but didn't say anything for a moment. Then: "What do you think?"

"What did they argue about?"

She pursed her lips. "Which one of them had the bigger ego. Man stuff."

"Right," I said. "But what did they argue *about*?"

She lowered her eyes. "I have no idea."

For some reason, it was just stupidly important that she give me a straight answer. But when I opened my mouth to push her into giving me the runaround yet again, I was interrupted by the sound of voices in the back hall. Flashlights swung around in all directions.

The tour of the super-secret basement had concluded. Not only had I missed it, but I hadn't made Marianne open up to me, either.

All I had was the sense that she wasn't telling me *something*.

Jim had assumed that Maddy had been telling the truth when she had accused me of breaking into everyone's houses, then denied that there was anything in his house that I would want.

Marianne had swerved around the topic of what Jim and my husband had almost come to blows about, and, in fact, had downplayed just how tense the situation had been.

And so had my husband.

If it had been about me—say, if Jim had called me a whore—Jack would have decked him and we would have left. If it had been about politics, Jack would have gone off about it endlessly for a couple of days about how stupid that so-and-so Jim was. Jack was a ranter. He was the cock of the yard and I loved him for it—but he couldn't have stopped himself from crowing.

The others marched into the room, laughing and saying, "Right?" They all sat at the table, sort of in the same groups as for the second cribbage game, but not quite.

Maddy was missing. Everyone else was there.

"Where's Maddy?" I asked. "Still lying down?"

Nick said, "I checked on her a few minutes ago. She told me she was sleeping and to mind my own business."

I rolled my eyes. "Told you, huh?"

Austin said, "Jim says the road is completely washed out now."

"Yeah," I said.

"Where were you?" he asked. "Walking around outside or something? See anything else?"

"Writing," I said.

"Uh-huh," Austin said. "In the dark, out in your car."

"On my laptop. I've had writer's block for a year. Since my husband died."

"Oh," Austin said. "Uh. Sorry."

Bob—*Bob*, of all people—said, "Hey, that's great. Good for you, writing again."

"Thanks," I said. I wondered whether he was a fan; earlier, he'd said he only read sci fi and fantasy. Or maybe he was himself a writer: it might explain a few things if so. The weird way he acted around me sometimes kind of felt like a younger writer fanboying around someone they admire. Almost. "Do you write, Bob? I didn't ask."

"A little," he admitted, as if it were a slightly shameful habit. "I mean, just enough to go, 'Wow, this is harder than it looks.' You know. I'm mostly a gamer."

When someone like Bob calls himself *a gamer* it means that he's a general geek: tabletop role-playing games like Dungeons and Dragons, video games, board games, strategy games, often card games and chess. The works. *Not* sports. I myself was something of a gamer, although I tended to avoid committing to anything on a regular basis now that I was a professional writer. Jack had been a video gamer—something slightly different. He played video games and was good at them, but didn't spend much time on any other types of games. He wasn't the kind of guy who enjoyed peeling the plastic off a new board game or sorting through three booklets of rules. He didn't buy the newest rule books or paint miniatures or go to geek conventions.

Jack was just the kind of guy who liked to shoot pixels in the head.

"Do you...write game materials?" I asked, guessing.

Sheepishly, he said, "I have a Dungeons and Dragons group down in Denver. I write the campaigns and stuff."

"I've been to a couple of Comic-Cons," I said. "Just the one in Denver. Although it's called something else now."

He nodded. "For...writer stuff?"

"Yeah. I've been on a couple of panels. Mostly I did it to get a free door pass so I could check things out. But mostly people at that kind of convention aren't interested in mysteries, unless you start talking about the horror elements, the dead bodies and stuff, so I decided against going back."

I wasn't exactly sure what I was trying to do other than make conversation. Ever since I had been accused of breaking into people's houses, something shifted inside me. Not just going from "not writing" to "writing," but something else. But I'm used to that while I'm writing: my subconscious is up to something. I just have to wait to find out what.

"I have friends who go every year," Bob was saying. "A lot of friends who are writers, or sellers, or both. But I like the smaller cons better. At a comic-con level event, you stop seeing fellow fans. The people just become this wall of meat."

"Wall of meat?" Sally asked, one eyebrow raised.

Egan said, "Comic-con is definitely a wall of meat. The one in San Diego is even worse. Smells worse, too."

Austin nodded. "And Gen Con."

Gen Con was a famous geek and gamer convention in Indianapolis in August, renowned (among other things) for the number of people who didn't bathe while they were there.

"And Gen Con," said Nick, Tony, Egan, and Bob, in a tone both worshipful and disgusted.

I said, "I was thinking about trying to get Jack to go to that."

They all looked at me. Disgusted, Jim said, "You're all a bunch of geeks," and the guys burst out laughing.

"Geeks, geeks!" Austin grunted.

Jim got up from the table and went into the living room, sitting in a chair next to Marianne. He spoke to her in a low voice; she answered in a murmur without looking up.

Meanwhile, Austin said, "I didn't know Jack was a geek."

"Sort-of geek," I said. "I grew up geek, but he didn't. He got into video games but didn't branch out."

"Ahhh..." Austin said, nodding. *He* knew the difference. "First person shooters."

"You'd think he would have, being a computer guy," Nick said. "Didn't he go to college?"

"No," I said. "He was in the Army for a while, got out, and was going to go into college but got married instead."

"To you?" Austin asked.

I rolled my eyes. "No, to his first wife, Amanda. She lives in Nebraska now. You know the type. Blonde hair dyed even blonder, sports jerseys, and beer."

"What happened?" Austin asked.

"She hooked up with an old boyfriend while he was TDY," I said.

"Ouch," said Austin. "But, dude. I have to ask. How did you hook up with a guy who wasn't a geek, if you're a geek? A writer geek, anyway?"

"You won't believe it. I met him at a LAN party," I said. "My boyfriend at the time dragged me along to play Wolfenstein Enemy Territory, and we hit it off while my boyfriend was frothing at the mouth and making excuses for why he would have kicked everyone else's ass, if only blah blah blah."

Tony laughed. "I think I know that guy."

Austin said, "Who, her ex-boyfriend?"

"No, your momma. Remember Ted?"

Austin, Egan, and Nick all said, "I remember Ted."

"Was his name Ted?" Austin asked.

"No," I said.

"So you dumped the ex and hooked up with Jack," Austin concluded. "Smart choice, in my opinion. Did you stop gaming together when you got married?"

"No," I said. "We still gamed. Mostly co-op, though. You can only play so much PVP together before you start having dreams about sniping them during an argument."

"Dude," the guys said. "She still games," Tony added. They all looked at me like I'd achieved goddess status.

I rolled my eyes. "...or you could try dating women who game."

Bob said, "I'm sorry you lost your husband, Liz. I don't know if I've said that. I didn't know he was such a good guy."

I gave him a look. He had spoken in a monotone, and now had a completely blank face. "He would have laughed to hear you call him a good guy, sure, but he really was. Or at least, if he was a bastard, he was *my* bastard. But thank you."

Sally looked up toward the ceiling, a faraway gaze staring far beyond the dark popcorn ceiling. "So that's what it was all about."

"What?" Austin asked.

Sally looked down at him. "None of your business, young man."

He rolled his eyes.

"Any of mine?" I asked.

Sally gave me a cynical half-smile, the kind of face that old-time movie stars used to make: a Katherine Hepburn face. "Anything's *your* business, if you make it your business. You're a writer."

"Touché."

"But I was thinking about the burglary. This isn't the first time I've had one, you know."

"No, I didn't," I said. "Was this before or after the serial killer?"

Sally stuck her tongue out at me. "If Maddy had been awake to hear that, she would have snorted coffee out her nose. This was before. *Long* before. It was a pervert."

The guys, including Bob, gaped at her and made incredulous noises like they couldn't believe that a pervert would ever had bothered with someone like her—but Wendy and I exchanged a glance between our two kitchen stools that said both *Of course she was a hottie at some point, she carries herself that way* and *Perverts will hit on anyone.* It was the mixed kind of look that I was used to sharing with other women—ever since I hit forty.

"I had just moved out of the college dorms and into a house with four or five other girls," Sally said. "This was in the Seventies. We reveled in our independence."

"Did anyone smoke pot?" Austin asked.

Sally lifted her eyebrows. "We drew a very liberal line at heroin." She laughed as Austin whistled. "But don't interrupt, that's all over and done with, and most of the time it was uppers and downers, depending on whether or not we had to study, and, honestly, it was one of those situations where most of us tired of it quickly, especially in light of the things that happened to people who *didn't* tire of it at all. After you've lost a few friends at such a young age due to overdoses, the scene tends to lose its charm. I suppose board games are an unexciting, but safer, replacement. But we were speaking of my pervert."

"*Your* pervert?" I asked.

"Yes, mine." Her eyes were back to staring through the ceiling. "I had a young man who followed me around. On campus, off campus. With friends, by myself, in grocery stores, you name it. He followed me. He'd asked me out once and I'd told him no; therefore, in his mind, it was perfectly healthy to follow me around. From a few of the things he'd said, little notes and during his supposedly-anonymous phone calls, I think he had decided that I hadn't said 'no.' I must have said 'yes,' and we were dating. In his mind, we were going steady. He was a bit demented. But I'm losing the thread of what I wanted to say...I had been burgled. One night, after a particularly difficult test, I had had enough. I shouted at him, the way you would shout at a stray dog who was following you around, looking for scraps. I made it clear in no uncertain terms that I was breaking up with him."

"But you weren't dating," Austin said.

"Do you think *he* understood that?" Sally retorted. "I told him—completely untrue, by the way—that I had been sneaking around behind his back and sleeping around with all sorts of men. I told him that I had chlamydia, syphilis, and typhoid fever. I told him that everyone else on campus was laughing at him behind his back at what a slut I was. You can imagine his reaction."

"Wow," said Egan. "Nope. Can't."

Sally laughed. "You are all *so* naïve. It's charming. The poor boy burst into tears and said that he *forgave* me."

I coughed out a laugh. "Oh, my God. I can totally see that. What on earth did you do then? Marry him, happily ever after, the story of your first husband, what?"

"You forget that this was supposed to be a story about burglary," Sally said. "No. He told me that he would forgive everything, that we could get over anything together. I had only played straight into his fantasy. He even told me that, if I was pregnant, we could marry and he would pretend to be the child's father. I told him that I was going to get an abortion, of course—I wasn't pregnant and wasn't about to become so just to prove a point—but that didn't throw him off one bit. What to do, what to do? I was at my wits' end. I stormed off, and he tried to follow me, sobbing. So I ducked into the nearest building, which happened to be the English hall, and told the secretary at the desk that I needed to make a confidential call. Of course the man followed me inside, sobbing. But that only worked in my favor, and the secretary showed me into a private office—without letting the young man follow me further inside. I was grateful, you can imagine. I called a girlfriend with a car and a driver's license, and she picked up a few things for me at our rented house and then came to pick me up. The two of us drove out of town—this was in San Francisco—and went to Las Vegas for the weekend."

"And while you were gone, he burgled your house?" Austin asked.

Sally chortled. "I called my roommates and told them to spread about the story that I'd tried to kill myself and was in a mental hospital."

"What!" Austin's chair scraped on the floor and almost fell down behind him.

"Dear pet," Sally said, "Haven't you been listening? Of course I did. The young man was shattered. He worried himself immensely for the entire weekend while I was enjoying myself at the casinos with my girlfriend. And, while we were gone, he broke into the house in order to get a memento."

I clicked my tongue. "In case you died from your suicide attempt."

Sally shot a finger-gun in my direction. "He was a sweet boy. Completely unhinged. But, in the context of his own little fantasy world, sweet. He took several pieces of underwear, a blouse of mine that I particularly liked, and a notebook that I had written in. And can you guess what was in the notebook?"

"No," I said. "Not a diary."

Sally wasn't the kind of woman who kept a diary—or at least, wasn't the kind of woman who left a diary lying around.

"Oh, it was a diary. It *was*. I'm a terrible person. The worst. I don't suppose that you've put me into any of your books yet, have you?" she asked suddenly. "Oh, what am I saying? Of course you *will*. I should tell you all my stories. The diary contained several entries—only twenty or so, very short—that were me amusing myself with a few little vignettes that I thought

I might pull together for an assignment in an English class. None of them were true, of course."

I closed my eyes, a flash of insight telling me what was coming next. Not that saying so would have stopped Sally from telling the rest of her story.

"What?" Austin asked. "What diary entries?"

"Oh, just a few little diary entries about how I had been planning to kill myself because of the fellow who was following me," Sally said. "They were brutal. Not the normal sort of thing you might expect, boo hoo, there's a *man* following me, what shall I do? No, I'd made up this rather Gothic sort of story where the love of my life had been taken away from me by an incestuous sister of his, and now that this fellow was following me around and trying to force himself on me, I might as well kill myself—as, even if my one true love was able to escape from his sister, he would think the worst: I had betrayed him with this idiot chemistry major, who was really the worst sort of man, both repulsive and evil. I think we had just finished *Wuthering Heights* in English class, and Gothics were very popular back then, women in nightgowns running shrieking from a dimly lit castle. You know what I'm talking about," she said to me directly, taking her eyes away from the popcorn ceiling and returning to the here-and-now.

"And?" I said.

"And he took that, too," she said.

"And?" I said.

"He killed himself," she announced. "Left a note begging my forgiveness and everything. And that was that."

The guys gasped, and Austin's chair went over with a thump onto the carpet as the two back feet hit the ridge at the edge of the tile.

Sally cackled until the tears ran down her face—*not* tears of regret, either.

"What do you think of that?" she asked, finally. "I'm an evil old woman, and I know it. When I was younger, I was only a little more brazen about it."

Austin hadn't hit his head on anything as he fell backward into the living room, fortunately—I don't know what we would have done, if he'd hurt himself. He lay there for a few moments, all the way through Sally's laughter and her outrageous statement, then said, in a tone of awe: "You're less brazen *now*?"

"Well, yes, obviously," Sally said. "I have my eye on the bigger picture *now*. If I had the wisdom back then that I have now, I wouldn't have tried to outfox obsession by acting even more strangely than he did. He simply didn't *care* how I acted; that was the whole point. I wasn't a person to him, but a sort of goddess, and he would have inflicted his sick little worship on me no matter what I did."

Austin was still too stunned to get up. Flat on his back, he said, "What would you have done?"

"Oh, ignored him, I suppose," Sally said, wiping her eyes. "Or arranged for him to find himself in a shallow grave in the woods."

Austin's mouth dropped open.

Jim, his voice hoarse, said, "Oh, like *that's* not brazen. You're just making this up, aren't you?"

Sally winked at him and struggled with her chair, trying to stand up. "Admittedly, I would have done something more subtle, if I wanted to get rid of someone. There are ways and ways to hurt someone. You don't have to use the ones that leave any sort of suspicions."

"Like what?" I asked.

Egan had gallantly stood up and helped hold Sally's chair so she could stand. She patted him on the arm. "Thank you, sir. A true gentleman. But it's not only us ladies who need help getting to our feet. Help your friend Austin up, too, while you're up."

Then she turned to me: "Looking for new murder methods for your books?"

"Always."

"May I suggest, then, the delights of doing *nothing*?"

I blinked and felt myself rock back on my kitchen stool. Wendy put a hand on my back to steady me.

"What?"

"Doing *nothing*, my dear," Sally said. "I've kept up with your books. They're serviceable but uninspired, the sort of work that a writer does before they've found their true *niche*. Your trusty little band of historians researches something, gets pulled into some drama by random killers, and use their historical research to learn a lesson that helps them solve the real-life case. Or vice versa. Sounds rather like a children's educational program, doesn't it?"

I felt my face go red and hot: it *did*, if she was going to be so cruel as to put it like that.

Sally faced me and held her hands out. They weren't young hands. They were definitely older and more weather beaten than even my forty-year-old ones were. But they weren't as gnarled and twisted as Maddy's hands. A couple of liver spots, thin skin, an absence of body fat on the fingers, heavy gold rings loose on the fingers.

But not *weak* hands, either.

Sally clutched her hands into fists, then moved them back and forth, miming their tugging a rope and pulling it tight. Then she opened one of her hands, letting go of the "rope," and the other hand flew to the side, released from its tension.

"Doing nothing," Sally said, her voice carrying clear and strong around the room. "Letting go. Letting someone destroy themselves of their own volition is one of the sweetest pleasures known to womankind. You little women spend all your time suppressing yourselves, making yourself smaller and less capable in order to make someone else look good. Then, suddenly—pah!" She mimed the same gesture. "One day, you snap. You don't even have to pick up a gun, climb into a clock tower, and start shooting people. All you have to do in order to get your revenge, is to *do nothing*. Let happen that which would have happened anyway."

She looked at Austin, who Egan had just helped to his feet. "That's what I meant, sweetie. What I should have done, if I knew then what I know now, was allow the man who was obsessed with me to eat himself alive, wreck and ruin his own life. As it was, I had to engage him several times, then give him a *push* to make him do what I wanted. But if I had done nothing, how much more satisfying."

"But what if he'd attacked you?" Austin asked.

Sally laid a finger on the side of her head and tilted it. "I see that I forgot to mention the secret to doing nothing. You don't literally take *no* action. I would have done whatever I needed in order to prevent his hurting me, of course. But I would have to *seem* to be doing nothing, and having no response to him whatsoever. Most of any action that I took would be to conceal that I had taken any action.

"Now, if you will excuse me, I would like to check on Maddy. She's been quiet and withdrawn for *quite* long enough."

Cheat Codes

Jim said, "What the hell was that crazy old bitch talking about?"

I frowned at him. If there was anyone whose behavior was being supported by another person in the room, it was Jim. What would happen, I wondered, if suddenly Marianne stopped doing her usual thing?

What *was* her usual thing? She was an excellent motorbike rider and a big reader. Something she had said earlier said to me that she was a bit of a thrill seeker, which made sense considering the motorbike riding. She was pretty, but in a made-up sort of way, carefully painted on. I always got a sense of restraint from her, too: I had never seen her without her face made up, and I had never seen her cut loose.

Which was kind of weird for a thrill-seeker.

It made me wonder: what kind of hold did Jim have on her, to make her act so differently than her nature dictated? Or was it Jim's hold? Some women carried around damage that had been inflicted on them during their early lives, damage that twisted their adult lives as well. Men, too, but men's damage didn't look like careful, cool restraint—concealment.

I was surprised to find myself saying, in answer to Jim's question, "Sally just likes to shock people. She has a new audience today, if you haven't noticed."

Jim snorted, content with my answer, which, if it wasn't exactly *wrong*, at least felt incomplete.

"I'll be damned," he said, "if I ever figure out what's going on tonight."

Wendy said, brightly, "There's always tomorrow. Does anyone need anything? I think we should try to get back to playing cards."

Austin said, "With two people out, that means you and Liz will have to play."

"I don't hate playing cards or anything," I said. "I'm just kind of drained from having to talk writing all weekend. Mentally drained."

"Talking about writing is exhausting?" Egan said.

"Talking about writing to people who are absolutely, positively convinced that they know how to write when they don't is exhausting," I said, correcting myself slightly.

"Ouch," Egan said, grinning. "I can see that. Doesn't anyone want to learn?"

"A few people," I said. "But mostly they want to have already written a book. They don't actually want to write." I let out a breath. I was carrying around a lot more anger after the convention than I'd realized. "No. That's unkind. They want to write. It's just that writing isn't what they imagined it would be. It doesn't feel like what it looks like on TV. So they panic and give up on it before they get to the fun part."

"But isn't that how it works for everything? If you're going to get good at something, then you have to go through a bunch of stupid lowbie shit to level up?"

He was speaking in gamer terms: in order to get good, you have to work at basic skillsets in order to move on.

"Yes," I said. "But if there's a better way to explain that to people, I don't know it. They want the secret cheat codes that unlock the higher levels, every time."

"Amen," Austin said.

Egan lifted an eyebrow. "My dude, you're the one who's always looking for cheat codes."

Austin said, "And even when I find them, you kick my ass. What's your point?"

"There aren't even any cheat codes for writing," Egan said.

I had been thinking while they bickered. I said, "You know what, it's even worse than how I described it. The people who are always looking for the cheat codes tend to put themselves into positions where they're teaching new players—new writers, I mean. College professors, writing coaches, online gurus. Everyone's like, 'Ten Easy Steps to Becoming a Professional Writer!' And half the time they're promoting a business set up to take advantage of newbies."

"Spawn camping," Egan announced.

Which, in this context, probably meant hanging out where the new players appeared in a video game and killing them for kicks.

"Right," I said. "Except while they're spawn camping, they're actively teaching the newbies bad advice on how to play."

"On purpose?" Egan asked.

"No, they seem to believe every word they say."

"What are they saying?" Austin asked.

"A lot of things," I said. "The one that truly cheeses me off is where they tell everyone to follow what is essentially the same plot line. You know how movies are all kind of the same lately?"

"Sure," Egan said.

"The same dude that caused that is causing the same thing in books," I summed up, overgeneralizing. "There's one dude, he used to work for Disney, he wrote down some stuff inspired by a college professor that wrote about a myth that showed up across cultures, basically the *Star Wars* story, and turned it into a universal template for making stories. *All* stories." I took a deep breath. "Sorry, rant over. Anyway, it isn't just a cheat code. It prevents writers from getting better. It's like convincing yourself that the only way to build a video game is to progress through levels to follow a storyline in a first-person shooter. Which kind of precludes the possibility of *Tetris*. Or *Street Fighter*. Or *BioShock*."

"Or *Minecraft*," Egan said. "Okay, I kind of get you. Where have all the weird books gone?"

"Where indeed," I said.

"Wasn't that just what Sally was giving you shit about?" Austin asked.

Egan rolled his eyes. "Way to get on someone's last nerve."

"I wasn't trying to piss anyone off," Austin said, grabbing his chair off the floor and putting it back on its feet.

"And yet, there you are," Egan said.

I was grateful not to have to try to keep up the pretense of discussion for a moment. It was a kick in the gut: Austin was right. I'd been doing exactly what I'd been complaining about. I'd been writing that kind of book. I wasn't doing it on purpose—but I was doing it, more or less.

I burst out with: "It really sucks being brainwashed, you know that? Austin wasn't wrong. And Sally wasn't wrong, either. I just don't want to hear it."

"Hey," Austin said. "Sorry."

"No worries," I said. "It's just hard." I got up and walked to the back door, passing Maddy's room as I went. The door was still closed. I went to the back door and opened it, watching the rain come down in the dark. I patted my pockets for the flashlight and found it. I aimed a light into the darkness and saw that my SUV was still sitting where I'd left it. I turned off my light again. It felt like I was on autopilot. I wasn't really thinking about what I was doing.

When I tried to put my flashlight back in my pocket, I noticed (finally) that I was still soaking wet.

What I'd intended to do when I'd first come back inside was grab my go-bag, get my dry clothes out, and change in the guest room. But I'd been interrupted by everyone coming up out of the secret basement.

Ah. I'd even forgotten about checking out the secret basement.

Quietly, I closed the back door and went into the guest bedroom, closing the bedroom door behind me.

The rattan goat head over the hidden doorknob was somewhat askew. I lifted the head off and set it aside on the bed, then turned the handle. The panel shifted a little, moving inward. I put my fingers into the crack to make sure the door didn't close on them, then rehung the goat head.

The inside of the door felt like the door on an RV, insulated and sealed, with industrial-style carpet all over the back to help absorb sound. I stepped over the bottom of the door frame, which was behind the baseboard, and stepped inside.

I had to slither around the end of the door in order to close it, first checking for a handle on the inside (there was one). For a moment I was in the dark and almost panicked.

Then I remembered I had a flashlight in my sodden pocket.

I pulled it out and lit up the area around me.

I was on top of a narrow landing. The walls were covered with ugly beige carpet tiles that didn't match the carpet on the floor in the bedroom. Which was stupid: what if you came out of the secret basement with a piece of off-colored carpet fluff on your shirt or something?

But I hadn't built the house. What did I know? I hadn't even suspected there was a secret basement down here in the first place.

I decided not to turn the lights on. I wanted to see the secret basement at its spookiest. I was afraid that turning the lights on would make the whole idea of a secret basement seem less cool, more ordinary.

The narrow landing led downward to a set of narrow, steep stairs, with a metal handrail on either side. The angle of descent was so steep that it looked like you'd need them, coming back up. I wondered how Maddy managed the stairs. Maybe she didn't. I walked down them. The stairs were carpeted with a metal strip at the end of each, for traction. They gave slightly underfoot, and I realized that they were made of metal under the carpet, almost a staggered ladder than a set of stairs. I turned around and checked the top of the stairs for any sign that the stairs could be raised or lowered, but didn't see anything. The stairs creaked a little as I went down them, but with all the carpet on the walls and the low ceiling overhead, I doubted you could hear anything from the main part of the house. Maybe if you stuck your head inside the cupboards along the wall in the kitchen; it seemed like that was where the stairwell would run, under the backside of the kitchen.

At the bottom of the stairs was another carpeted door, with the same style of doorknob. I opened it out onto pitch-black darkness.

For a moment I turned off my flashlight and stood there. I tried to sit down on the bottom step of the stairs, but the stair treads were too shallow to sit on.

Darkness swallowed me up.

It was a strange feeling. The last time I'd gone to a cave underground (over a year ago, and with Jack), the tour guide had tried to give us a little bit of what it feels like to be in absolute darkness by having all the lights in the tunnel shut off. "Don't worry, this will only last a minute. But it will be the longest, darkest minute of your life." Of course the first thing some asshole did was pull out her cell phone and take a photo. Not a flash photo. But you could still see the light of her screen reflected on her face.

Jack waited until the woman had gone around another bend in the tunnel, cut his finger on a pocket knife, then went up behind her and dripped a bead of blood down the back of her shirt. She reached around to feel what was on the back of her neck and screamed.

By then, Jack had fallen back beside me, completely straight-faced and keeping his hands in his pockets. Me, I struggled to keep it together for the entire rest of the tour. Fortunately there wasn't much more of it. But that was Jack.

And now he was gone.

When you love someone for long enough, you start to rebuild your brain around them. You rely on their strengths. If you're smart, you start using them as your inspiration to become stronger yourself.

But I'm not that smart.

Since Jack's death, I felt like I was missing something. I wasn't just missing Jack. I was missing some part of me that used to make me human. What was it? I couldn't remember; it must have atrophied. Whatever it was gave color to the world. It made food taste good. It made me want to wake up in the morning. It made me want to write.

I had thought it was gone. But it wasn't. Proof being, I had just spent an hour writing in the SUV in the middle of a deafening thunder- and hailstorm.

It must just have been atrophied.

And...what? Needed time to heal?

Had it healed on its own?

I felt my mouth press into a straight line. I knew that whatever was wrong with me hadn't healed on its own. Or at least not completely.

Something had reset it, restarted it.

And it had happened here, tonight.

But what?

The Big Secret

I sat and stared into the darkness for what felt like a long time, coming to no conclusions but kind of enjoying the feeling of having my subconscious chew on the problem for me. It felt like I was in the middle of a good writing session. My muse was in charge, and all I had to do was write down the words it fed to me—eventually.

But after a while I started to get bored with it. I'm actually really bad at being bored. Just terrible. I think most people who read are. We're so bad at being bored that all we can do to handle the boredom is escape into a book. Or a game. Gamers are as bad as readers, as far as I can tell. I'd tried meditation a couple of times, at the advice of a therapist who seemed like a nice woman but was ten years younger than me, pretty, and who had never married. After a few sessions of watching me try to meditate, we mutually agreed that I wasn't ready for it yet and I'd be better off swimming or jogging on a regular basis. I negotiated it down to long walks with my cell phone and a voice transcription program to talk out story problems. We declared it a victory and went out for sushi and talked books after our final session. I'm a much better acquaintance than client. I like her. It's one of those adult friendships where you both mostly just admire each other from a distance on social media and treasure the few times you can sneak away to used bookstores with each other.

I promised myself I would call her, sooner rather than later, and turned on my flashlight, somehow managing to reflect the bright beam back into my face. I winced and closed my eyes.

But from my glimpse I had seen that this was no "cavern measureless to man," but a carpet-covered cellar.

Eyes shut, I decided I had imagined what I had seen, aimed the flashlight at the floor this time, and turned it back on.

I was immediately disappointed.

As soon as I turned on the light the second time, the smell hit me: mildew, damp synthetic rubber-backed carpet, cement dust that had never really cleared from the air of the basement. Damp pressboard furniture.

The floor was the same blue carpet tiles as the guest bedroom upstairs; the walls and ceiling, the same beige carpet as the stairwell. There were water stains on the carpet covering the ceiling overhead. Several covered vents interrupted the stretch of ceiling nearby. On the floor lay four sleeping bags. The rest of the furniture mainly consisted of bean bags, a card table whose legs had been half-sawn off and taped with duct tape so that the tabletop lay within easy reach of the bean bags, and an old entertainment center with a flat-screen TV and nice Bose speakers hanging from wires run along the ceiling.

The shadows danced as I swung the flashlight back and forth around the room.

This wasn't all it was, was it? *This* was the big secret?

This was it?

It felt like someone had stabbed me in the chest.

Some basement.

Some secret.

Suddenly, I felt tired. An exhaustion of the soul. I walked over to one of the beanbag chairs, curled up on it, and closed my eyes. The beanbag was just big enough for me to do it. My wet clothes stuck to my skin and left the leatherette surface of the chair feeling gross and clammy, like a dead person's skin.

Out of my guts came grief.

For a year I had been grieving—or so I'd thought. But no. I'd only been letting myself feel the first little edges of grief, seeping around the walls I'd built against grief. At first I wept so hard that I could barely make a sound. My chest hurt. I wanted to sleep—I wanted to be dead.

Slowly, sobs began to escape from me. A peep here, a groan there. Then a continuous stream of ugly noise: gulping, puking, wretched sounds. I lay with my arms wrapped in a loose, empty circle in front of me, sometimes with my head between them, sometimes leaning on one arm.

Then came the words.

I begged Jack for forgiveness. For what, I didn't know. Letting him die? No, that wasn't it.

Once again, I found my hands suddenly gripping tight around empty air, as if trying to wring someone's neck. A desperate need for revenge tore through me. Then I went back to begging Jack's forgiveness.

Although it seemed to take a thousand years, the crying jag soon passed through me, a storm that blew through. The only difference was the severity of the emotion. Or that I hadn't bothered to restrain it.

Why should I? I was in a sound-proofed basement. Nobody could hear me.

I sat up, face dripping, and went looking for a tissue. A piece of toilet paper would have done.

I soon found one, in a pocket toilet underneath the stairs. I almost missed the door; it was covered with carpet, and only the sudden interruption of another of those door handles gave it away.

The bathroom was small, creepy, and filled with spider-webs—including one on the toilet. I guessed that the guys went upstairs rather than use this one. No tissues. I ripped off a few squares of toilet paper, tossed it in the trash (the thought of wiping spiderwebs onto my face made me wince), tore off a longer section, and used it to wipe my face.

Then I walked back to the door to the stairs and found the light switch. I turned it on, and several fluorescent bulbs flick-ered to life around the edges of the room. I walked around the room. It was smaller than I had expected, and certainly didn't fill up the basement. If the stairs went underneath the kitchen, then I supposed that the main room didn't go much past the edge of the carpet upstairs. I walked back to the stairs intending to follow the line of the ceiling down into the room.

As soon as I opened the door to the stairs, the lights popped and went out.

I cursed myself for shorting out a fuse, then stupidly flicked the lights on and off for a second. Nothing. Idiot! I sighed and leaned against the wall, unintentionally forcing the door closed.

A split second after the door closed, the lights flickered back on.

I blinked. Then screwed around with the door for half a minute, working out that the lights had been set to cut out as soon as the door was opened. I wondered if the light in the stairwell worked in the same way.

Then I went, *Wait. Isn't the power supposed to be out?*

Why, yes.

It was.

In fact, the power *was* out. When Jim and I had gone outside to check the flooding at the bottom of the drive, the darkness—except during lightning flashes—had been so great as to seem surreal, cutting us off from the rest of the world.

Now, people aren't packed in cheek to jowl in the mountains, that's true, but it's not like you can't see the yard lights of your neighbors, and your neighbor's neighbors, and so on. Normally the mountains are pleasantly dotted with little constellations of yard lights.

The power all over the mountain was out.

Therefore, the secret basement had a secret power source, a generator or something. Did Maddy have a generator that I knew of? Most people did, in case the power went out—but you didn't really think of them until winter blizzards. Portable generators were loud, but you could get a model installed that was more or less the size of an air conditioning unit and ran off the same propane tank that most everyone up here used to heat their homes anyway. Pretty efficient.

I couldn't hear anything running down here. I walked around the perimeter again, stopping to listen here and there, but not catching the purr of a generator. I knew it would be a bad idea to leave a propane generator in a sealed basement. But I still checked.

Nothing.

I walked around in a circle, dragging my fingers along the wall. The carpet along the walls was longer and shaggier than the stuff on the floor. More sound absorbent.

I felt something catch under my fingers and stopped, raking them along the strands again.

Yes, there was definitely something there.

I traced the line to the top and bottom of the wall. Was it just a carpet seam? I looked around. Down in the basement, there were no convenient rattan goat heads to conceal a handle. In fact there was no wall art at all. Just the carpet, a light switch, and the handles to the bathroom and upstairs doors. I looked behind the TV, which was the only thing pressed up against the wall. Nothing other than an electrical plug.

There were two other outlets. I wedged my fingernails behind them to make sure they weren't fake. Nothing came loose.

I walked around and around: there had to be something else down here.

Where was the generator?

Why did the main room only take up half the basement?

Why couldn't I figure it out?

———

A quick check on my phone established that it was about one a.m. How had it become so late? Or was it early? I tried to add the time up in my head. The card game, the power going out, checking the road, typing on my laptop, searching the basement...no matter how I tried to figure it, the time didn't come out right. Unless I hadn't spent that much time in the basement after all.

I went to the door and shut out the light, closing the carpeted door at the bottom of the stairs behind me, then walked slowly up the carpet-covered metal stairs, feeling the slightest give and sway to them. At the top of the stairs I paused. It was pitch dark in the stairwell. There *ought* to be a way to find out whether it was safe to open the door, but if there was one, I couldn't see it.

Automatically, I batted at the place on the wall where I remembered seeing a light switch. The light was off. My action was on autopilot: years of being yelled at to "turn off the goddamned lights!" and decades of reinforcing that habit on my own.

The light switch was down. My hand skidded off it.

Then, again without thinking, I flipped the switch to the "up" position.

Nothing happened.

I turned it off again. Then turned it on, then off.

I decided that either it had burned out, or that it was hooked up to the main power source rather than the generator.

Then the light blinked.

Once.

Twice.

Three times.

I clapped a hand over my mouth to keep my guffaw from echoing around the stairwell. The light in the stairwell had *nothing* to do with lighting the way down the stairs. It was a signal light. I fumbled around on the back side of the carpeted door until I found the handle (it was in that weird position opposite the rattan goat head on the other side of the wall), then slowly opened the door and stepped into the guest room.

Of course everyone in the house knew about the secret basement now; they had all just come out of it. There was no point in hiding the fact that I was leaving it.

And yet it was satisfying, hiding the fact that I had just done so. And it made me wonder: what signal had the light switch given? And where? Had I just made a perfectly obvious light flash in the dark house?

And who had answered it?

Mona Lisa Smile

When I stepped out of the guest room (the door was still closed), everyone was sitting in the living room half of the main room. Jim sat opposite Marianne in an armchair; three of the four boys sat on one of the couches, and Bob and Nick sat on a love seat. By "everyone" I didn't mean "everyone." Sally and Maddy were still out of the room in Maddy's bedroom, and Wendy was still on her stool in the kitchen.

It was always easy to take Wendy for granted. But it came to me in a flash that it was she who had answered my signal—somehow. The others in the great room were all staring at their phones, a bright glow in each face. I could hear the faint *beep beep boop* of phone games from several phones. The only exception was Nick, who held his phone in his lap and was looking at me, judging my expression or body language or something.

"What's up?" I asked. "You look like a bunch of Millennials on your phones."

It was a lame joke. Everyone ignored me.

I walked over to Wendy and bumped her with my hip. "Hey," I said.

"Hey." Her plain face gave me a smile, then went back to its previous non-expression.

I sat next to her and leaned forward on the kitchen island with my elbows. "Why isn't anyone going to bed?" I asked. "Is it because no one has solved the mystery of why I broke into all those houses?"

That earned me another smile. Once again, no one other than Nick seemed to notice that I'd said anything.

"Is Maddy okay?" I asked.

Wendy answered, speaking softly. "Sally is talking to her. I think she's really upset."

I licked my lips. "Wendy…" I wasn't sure what I wanted to say. The urge to say *something* was there. But I hadn't quite figured out where the urge was leading. It made my throat too tight to speak for the moment, at any rate.

She lifted an eyebrow. My eyes had adjusted enough to the darkness that I could see her expression more or less clearly. But it didn't inspire whatever it was I was trying to ask her about to come to the surface.

I shook my head, leaned back, and ran my hands along the edge of the counter, as if in nervous agitation. Then I flipped my wrists around and ran my fingers under the edge.

They only just brushed the edge of something when Wendy grabbed the wrist nearer to her. She pursed her lips, then shook her head.

I nodded.

When I looked back into the living room, everyone was back on their phones. Even Nick.

It almost seemed as though he were avoiding my gaze, as a matter of fact.

I sat there in the dark, watching everyone else play games on their phones—or read, in Marianne's case. The thing that I wanted to ask stayed stuck in my throat. The words were trapped. I struggled to figure out what words so desperately wanted out that they had to choke themselves into silence. Finally I stood up.

"I'm going to check on Maddy," I said to Wendy.

She put her hand on my arm. "Wait."

"Wait for what?"

"Sally's talking to her now."

"And then what?" I asked. "After she comes out, it's my turn?"

"If you like."

Annoyed, I walked over to the fridge and opened it without taking anything out: the last refuge of someone who doesn't know what they want. Again, lifelong habit took over, and I grabbed a plate of cheese slices and brought it out, dropping it in front of my kitchen stool. It was half-eaten and covered with plastic, which I stripped off and ruthlessly wadded into a tangled ball that would be a real pain to straighten out again. I grabbed a slice of supermarket cheddar and stuffed it into my mouth.

Let the stress eating begin.

As far as I could tell, this whole evening had gotten Maddy nowhere. Why had she accused me, knowing that I hadn't done it? Because she wanted to distract everyone from the real culprit.

If she had wanted to distract everyone from the real culprit, either she knew who it was, or she didn't, I reasoned.

And...wait. How had she known it wasn't me?

I narrowed my eyes and looked around the room.

Both Wendy and I had been framed as culprits. Wendy initially had been introduced as one, but quickly dismissed.

Then the victims of the crimes—Bob, Sally, and the Griffiths—had also been framed.

The only people who hadn't been set up as the culprits by whatever subtle, manipulative magic that only Maddy seemed to be able to work were the boys and Maddy herself.

I searched my memory. There was something about the boys...that was right. They were at Maddy's house because they were all in trouble, or some of them were in trouble, but I hadn't found out what.

"Wendy," I said, "What were Nick and his friends in trouble about?"

Lowering her already faint murmur to a positive whisper, Wendy said, "They were *arrested.*"

"For what?"

"Breaking and entering."

The hair stood up on the back of my neck.

"They broke into someone's house?"

"Nick's ex-girlfriend's house," Wendy said. "But it wasn't what you might think. The girl's current boyfriend was the one who called the cops on them. It was all a mistake. The boyfriend had kicked the ex-girlfriend out of her own house and changed the locks, can you believe it? And he not only refused to get out of the house but wouldn't let her have anything in the house. And when she had left, she had left behind all kinds of important things."

"Why didn't she call the cops on the boyfriend?" I asked, appalled.

Wendy shrugged. "Because he beat the shit out of her and threatened to shoot her? She left in a hurry. At any rate the boys broke in and got the things she needed. The boyfriend had set up a security cam. He called the cops on them and gave them her address. They were brought in and questioned, then Maddy got them all out on bail and made them drive up here so tempers didn't go any higher than they were already."

"What about the ex-girlfriend?" I asked. I hoped she hadn't gone back to the crazy boyfriend.

"Oh, she got flown out of state, back to her grandparents' house in Illinois," Wendy said. "Maddy said that Nick said that she was doing all right back there. At least now she has her purse and social security card and things."

"What's happening about the boyfriend?" I asked. "Is anyone doing *anything* to get him arrested, or locked up, or what?"

Wendy shook her head. "All I know is that the boys have promised not to do anything until after tonight."

After tonight. Which meant that whatever Maddy was going to do about it depended on how tonight came out. A favor for a favor, perhaps?

"Does Nick have a car?" I asked.

"Nick has a car, and Egan has a van," said Wendy.

I made sure nobody was looking at me, then asked, "And where were they, on June fourth, fifth, and sixth?"

That got me what was neither more nor less than a Mona Lisa smile.

I took a breath, then ate another slice of cheese.

Who had robbed Bob, Sally, and the Griffiths's homes?

The boys, at Maddy's instigation, no doubt.

I had no proof.

I hoped that the cops wouldn't find any, either.

"What are you up to?" I asked myself.

"Cleaning house," Wendy said, in a voice that sounded almost grim. I glanced at her. Whatever emotion had grabbed her had already passed, and she gave me another blank sort of smile.

Whatever it was that had just happened, the tightness in my throat had passed, lowering downward into my chest, as tight as a panic attack.

Or a broken heart.

From the back of the house, a door opened. Maddy's bedroom door. Everyone looked up but Jim and Marianne.

After a moment, Sally walked into the room, looked around at everyone on their phones—and all the comfy spots being occupied. Her shoulders dropped, and she started walking toward the kitchen table. She looked tired. Her eyes were only half-open and her hands were doing that thing that sometimes older women's hands do, where the palms look like they're about to fold in half the long way.

Nick started to stand up. Austin, too.

But the first one to speak was Marianne.

"Take my spot," she said, turning off her phone screen. "I wanted to ask Maddy something."

"Ask her what?" Jim asked, sounding sharp.

Marianne ignored him and climbed out of the recliner as elegantly as a beauty-pageant contestant being examined on her poise. Sally lowered herself into the chair a little more awkwardly, sighing as she sat.

"How is she?" I asked.

"Just about cried out," Sally said, twisting in the recliner to talk to me over her shoulder. "She says she's sorry that she tried that dumb stunt earlier, by the way. She was trying to make the guilty party confess."

Softly, the door of Maddy's bedroom closed.

I blinked. "And?"

"Well, unless someone confessed while I was in the bedroom listening to her sob, it didn't work."

"I don't think the person behind the thefts is here," I said. "I mean, that's what would happen if this was a murder mystery novel. But that's not how things work in real life. You don't just call all the suspects together and announce who dunnit. You call the police."

Sally tilted her head to the side, then turned away from me. "That's *if* you want to bring the police in," she said. "Sometimes it's better to handle these things on your own."

"I don't see how," I said. "Unless you're planning to do something illegal yourself."

Nick said, "Sometimes there isn't time to go to the cops. Sometimes you have to do something yourself."

"Are you sure?" I asked. "What if you end up putting someone in even more danger by not going to the cops?"

Visibly, Nick winced.

All right, I'll admit it: I was in a nasty mood just then. My chest hurt. I grabbed another piece of cheese.

"It's a difficult decision sometimes," Sally said. "Sometimes you put things off, and put them off again, and again, until finally it's too late to have called the cops when you should have. What then? Do nothing? What if it takes time to accept that you should have done something in the first place?"

I sighed. It didn't really sound like Sally was talking to me. She waited to see if I would answer her. I didn't. She pulled out her phone and started poking at a game on it, one that flashed red and blue splotches on her face as she played.

I sank back into my funk, understanding that I'd missed my chance to see Maddy. Now I'd just have to wait until Marianne came back out again.

So Maddy had had the houses robbed. Why?

Bob's house, the Griffiths' house, Sally's house.

What had been taken? Mostly paperwork.

What sort of paperwork would be at Bob's house of any interest? Paperwork related to the security company, probably. His house had been the first, on the fourth of June.

Then what?

Sally's house, on June fifth.

What sort of paperwork would she have of interest?

Something related to real estate.

Then, on June sixth, the Griffiths' had been burgled.

What sort of paperwork would *they* have had that Maddy wanted?

Jim was retired.

They would have paperwork related to their charity work, I supposed. Were they embezzling funds? For a while earlier that evening, I had almost started to suspect that Jim was the thief, and that Marianne had been covering up for his early return back to Colorado from Las Vegas. But if Jim wasn't the thief—and the boys were—then I wasn't sure. What was there even to cover up? If he was embezzling, then having him come back to Colorado early wouldn't mean anything. I didn't know. Maybe they had just fought and Jim had come back early for that reason, and they were covering it up because that was what some couples did. No matter how bad things got, it was all so much dirty laundry that nobody wanted aired out in public. Some people were just like that.

Or had Jim come home early from Vegas at all? I still didn't know.

Maddy didn't like Jim. Whatever she had had the boys steal—assuming this whole chain of supposition wasn't complete bullshit—wouldn't have been to benefit *him*.

My mouth dropped open and a chill rushed over my skin. I stood up, made my way to the front door, and picked up my go-bag, the one with my change of clothes in it. I was shivering. It wasn't the cold. By then, my wet clothes had more or less warmed against my skin.

No: it was the thought that Maddy had wanted me here tonight for no apparent reason other than to serve as a distraction.

No *apparent* reason.

"I'm going to change clothes," I said.

"You go for it," Austin said, not looking up from his phone.

Tony said, "Dude. I thought you changed clothes earlier."

I went into the bathroom, stripped down, and put on my dry clothes.

What if all of this had been set up to benefit *me*?

THE THINGS YOU KEEP FOR YOURSELF

Finally in dry clothes, I stepped out of the bathroom at the same time that Marianne left Maddy's bedroom, both of us softly closing the doors behind us and looking up at the same time. I locked gazes with her; to my surprise, this time, she didn't drop her eyes, but instead stared into mine.

She said "The rest is up to you" and walked down the hallway to the main room.

Passing her and coming toward me were Nick and Egan. Nick said, "Hey, tell Maddy that we're going out to check the road again."

I patted my pocket, but the keys weren't in it. I had forgotten to take them out of my wet pants. I had stuffed the wet clothes into a plastic bag from under the sink. I bent over to sort through them, then handed my keys to Nick.

"What are these for?" Egan asked.

"So you don't have to walk in the rain," I said.

"Thanks," Nick said. "We'll be sure to leave your SUV right where we found it when we're done."

"Just don't roll off the mountain," I joked.

Egan said, "Oh, hey, the rain sounds like it's dying down a little anyway."

"Good," I said. "Maybe we'll be able to get out of here soon. I'm kind of done with having everyone cooped up here in the house together."

An angry argument erupted from the other room: Austin and Jim.

I said, "And by 'everyone' I mean Jim."

Nick said, "You'll still have to drive him home, won't you?"

I sighed. "At least I can get him out of everyone else's hair. That's something."

Nick nodded, and the two boys opened the back door and stepped out into the rain. It *did* seem as though it were dying down a little. At least the hail had stopped, by the sound of it. I got a glimpse of little white drifts of ice pellets washing across the gravel. Then the door closed behind them. I turned toward Maddy's bedroom door and let myself inside.

It was pitch black in the room. I turned on my flashlight and swung it around the room.

Maddy was gone.

I blinked.

Maddy's bedroom was the kind of place that a little girl might imagine for herself when she was about eight. She had a white wrought-iron bedstead with a decidedly frilly pink patchwork quilt on top and about seven million pillows. Her dresser—white-painted wood—was topped with a rectangular ivory crocheted doily and an endless sea of photographs. A silver tree held earrings in tiny holes in the branches, and rings at the tips. The walls were pink. The floor had a ridiculous, long-tufted, bright pink rug that looked like someone had skinned a Muppet and spread it out like a bear skin. A silver-framed mirror rested between the closet door and the dresser, a little tarnished. I looked at myself inside it and found my edges a little softer than usual.

I looked inside the closet. It was full of Maddy's dresses and cardigans, brighter and more assertive than the room would have indicated on its own. Lots of bright red and navy blue. And no Maddy.

I sat on the edge of the bed.

Of course, I thought. The reason that I couldn't find an entrance to the rest of the secret basement, the reason that I can't find Maddy now, is that there's another door to the other half of the secret basement.

Why not?

I couldn't think of a reason to split a secret basement in half—but I couldn't think of a reason not to, either. *Two* secrets. *Two* mysteries to be solved.

One obvious one.

One less so.

One secret to let other people "discover."

One secret to keep for yourself.

I looked behind the mirror and the dresser; I looked inside the closet and flipped the light switches on and off. I opened the drawers, I twisted the knobs, I checked the bedposts.

Nothing.

If I had to pass the test of finding the second secret door to the other half of the basement, I had failed it, and I didn't have a lot of hope of not failing it anytime soon. It was dark and after midnight and my heart was wrung out. Too many things had happened.

I left my bag of wet clothes on the floor and lay down on the bed, resting my head on lace-edged quilted pillows that scratched against my face, closed my eyes, and went to sleep.

In other words, I gave up.

———

I woke up not too much later, at the slam of the back door as the boys came back in. "Hey!" Egan shouted. "The lights are back on!"

From inside Maddy's bedroom, I couldn't tell. After screwing around with all the light switches, I had put them all in the "off" position, just in case the power *did* come back on. I hadn't wanted Maddy to have to race around the house, tutting about her wasted electricity.

I lifted my head a little; under the bedroom door spilled a thin thread of warm, yellow light from the hallway.

"We know! They came on while you were outside," Bob called to Nick and Egan from the living room.

I sat up. The short nap had done me some good, it felt like. Something had broken loose. It felt like one of those writing moments where I had been stuck on something in a book and, after a lot of stomping around and complaining to other writer friends, I had been hit by inspiration that had totally derailed my original plans but would work out better anyway.

It was a nice feeling, but also bittersweet. I swung my legs down onto the floor and fumbled around, looking for my phone. I couldn't remember taking it with me into the bedroom; I must have left it in the bathroom. I had been using the little flashlight to look around Maddy's bedroom, not the phone light. I scowled at myself in the mirror opposite the bed: *You're so irresponsible!* I didn't think that anyone would have stolen my phone, but I've always had the bad habit of leaving things lying around and completely forgetting to go back for them later. My dad used to call me a reverse kleptomaniac.

I got up and went into the bathroom. The brightness of the hallway lights made me blink.

My phone was indeed on the back of the toilet seat. I snorted in relief, then washed my face in the sink and went back out to the living room. Everyone was still sitting in their separate worlds, consulting their phones. Apparently the wifi wasn't back up yet. Maddy's computer set-up was in a back corner of the living room behind a folding divider screen, dark wood with a white paper backing. I could see Bob's butt sticking out past the edge of the screen as he bent over the computer. The monitor came on, throwing his silhouette onto the paper of the screen. I suppressed a chuckle.

"How are the roads?" I asked.

"Better," Nick said.

"Do you think I can drive across?" I asked.

"Probably," Nick said. "I mean, it would be better if you waited until morning. But if you gotta get out of here, now's okay if you're careful. I wouldn't want to ride the bikes down. There's a big dip where the water washed out the gravel around the culvert."

"Are you sure? Is it safe to drive?" I asked again.

He shrugged. "The water's gone down and the culvert seemed pretty solid." He dug around in his pocket and tossed me my keys. I caught them in midair; they were warm. "We didn't go all the way down to the paved road, just to the culvert."

I turned to Jim and Marianne, who were sitting beside each other in the recliners. "So. Do you want to get out of here?"

"Hell, yes," Jim said, getting to his feet. "I've had about enough of this kangaroo court business."

Funny; he wasn't the one who had been on trial: I was. He stretched out the small of his back, his face blank. It was an eerie look, actually. His eyelids were wide open, almost weirdly so, so wide that you could see almost his entire pupils. His lips were narrow and flat, expressionless. I noticed that he didn't have a lot of lines on his face: no frown lines between his eyebrows or around his lips, no laugh lines at the corners of his eyes. Didn't he ever make a face? Or was the face he made around people something that he only put on when others were looking?

Marianne said, with perfectly unconcerned blandness: "I think I'll stay."

"What's wrong with you?" Jim demanded.

"I don't feel like it," Marianne said.

"You don't *feel* like it?" he demanded.

"No. I'm very tired, and I feel that driving home in this weather is not worth the risk."

I frowned at her. Just what had she and Maddy talked about?

"What about me?" he asked.

"You can do what you like," she said. "I don't think Liz should have to drive you. Why don't you ask Bob to drive you?"

"Why should I?" he demanded.

I yawned hugely, then said, "You know, I think you're right. I don't feel like going out. I almost fell asleep in Maddy's room just now."

Wendy's head snapped toward me. I walked over to her and sat beside her on the other kitchen stool.

Bob straightened up from behind the screen. "You don't want me to drive you anywhere," he said. "I've been, uh. Sneaking drinks all night." He pulled a steel flask out of a pocket on the leg of his cargo pants and waggled it back and forth. Liquid—and not very much of it—sloshed from inside.

I gave him a narrow-eyed stare. I hadn't smelled any alcohol on him, and I hadn't caught him drinking at all. Had he just been carrying the flask around his pants to be "cool"? Was he just using it as an excuse?

Jim said, "Well, I'm not going to stick around. Liz, give me your keys. You can come and pick up your SUV in the morning."

I shook my head. "No, Jim. I don't let other people drive it. You're not on my insurance."

He stamped his foot. "What the hell? Someone give me a vehicle."

No one volunteered.

Marianne said, "Why not drive your bike?"

"Are you insane, woman? Not in this weather."

"Or you could walk," she said. "It's not far."

"It's still hailing!" he said, although the drum of ice on the roof had stopped.

Before anyone could answer him, the door of Maddy's room opened softly. I turned my head. So did Marianne and Sally, from the living room.

Maddy's hair was mussed and her dress a little rumpled. She hobbled a little as she walked, as if she'd twisted an ankle.

What would happen to her if she fell in the basement? Who would find her? I wondered, and shuddered.

She gave us a little wave. "I'm sorry, I seem to have fallen asleep for a little bit," she said. "How is everything?"

Jim stared at her like she was holding a gun at him. At least, he went rigid and balled his hands up; his back was to me, so I couldn't actually see his face.

One foot lifted, taking him a step closer to her, and I got up, grabbing something on the kitchen island in front of me and making a hissing noise between my clenched teeth.

I wasn't the only one. Nick and Egan were still standing near the end of the hallway; they stepped toward Maddy, obviously on guard. Austin and Tony got up from the couch, both of them terribly silent in that suddenly-quiet room. You could barely hear their stockinged feet on the carpet.

Marianne said, "Why don't you just go home, Jim? However you want to go. But *go*."

Sally started to chuckle.

Maddy said, "Unless Liz wants to drive you home, of course. Your choice."

I closed my eyes. A chill ran down the back of my neck, spreading down my arms and legs, leaving my fingers and toes almost numb with cold. I swallowed. My chest tightened and my throat closed until it felt almost as though I were having a heart attack. Three women, friends, people I'd known for years, and I felt frozen to the bone with the terror of them.

There was no mystery. This was not a whodunnit. This was three women conspiring together to destroy a man they hated, and making *me* be their judge.

If I wanted to save Jim's life, I had to get in my SUV and risk my own. Or we could all just let Jim make his own choices and face his own consequences, instead of dumping them on the rest of us.

Deep breath, eyes open, I said:

"Let him ride home, he wants to leave so bad."

THE EUMENIDES

Jim turned around slowly, looking at me. Whatever face he had made at Maddy, he had erased it. It was back to that unnerving blank look. All normal human expression had been erased.

His lip curled: an involuntary sneer. Then his face went blank again.

I licked my lips, glad that the kitchen island was between us.

I said, "You did something to Jack's bike."

No reaction.

"You did something to his bike," I repeated. "Before the night he died. That's what this is all about."

Wendy's hand reached for mine under the countertop, took my hand and squeezed it.

"The burglaries," I said. I felt short of breath, almost choking. "Your house, Bob's house, Sally's house. They were to gather information. Sally must have had blackmail information. She's always watching everyone. Bob works for the security company that covers your house. Nothing was stolen but papers from your house—but your computer could have been broken into. And then tonight. We've all been brought here together. To have it out."

Maddy said, "I'm sorry, Liz. I didn't realize...that it would hurt you so much."

My hands were shaking. I was still clutching whatever I'd picked up from the island. I looked down. I was holding a paring knife. I forced myself to drop it, then push it over to Wendy, who picked it up and put it in the knife block on the counter against the back wall. Then she took my hand and squeezed it, held it gently.

Jim visibly straightened up, almost standing on tiptoe, and growled, "I don't know what you're talking about."

He was literally looking down at me, using social engineering on our physical positions so that he would appear to dominate the conversation. He was raising his voice, and denying that what any of us said made any sense. He was *manipulating* me. Trying to pressure me into dropping the conversation.

He was used to getting his way.

It wasn't proof that my intuition was correct. But his reaction wasn't exactly consistent with innocence, either.

Sally said, "It's true about the blackmail information. I have something on everyone. I have digital photographs of Jim's bike parked beside your house the day that Jack died. I saw him pull up and thought, 'Well, now, isn't that interesting?' But I didn't say anything. I never do, you know, unless I think I can get something out of it."

I glanced at her. She stiffened in her recliner, gripping the arms of it. Her lower lip tightened. I wondered what expression I had on my face. I decided it didn't matter. I felt like I didn't have a face. I was beyond numb.

I looked back toward Jim. His nostrils flared. I felt some expression spread across my lips, not a smile. Something involuntary.

Bob cleared his throat. "I...I didn't hack into my company's security system. Someone else did that. Nick or Egan, maybe."

Tony said, "It was me."

"Uh..." Bob said hoarsely. "Anyway. It was...you're wrong, Maddy. Jim didn't kill Jack. It was me."

Now I looked at him, and he took a step sideways, half-concealing himself behind the divider screen. Then he breathed in, gathering himself, and took the edge of the screen, hands shaking, and pulled it away from the computer behind it.

The glow from Maddy's computer screen seemed to fill the room.

Bob had pulled up an image on Maddy's screen, a foreshortened stretch of black truck hood with a winding mountain road in front of it. The image was frozen. The sky was dark and gray. The windshield showed double arcs from the windshield wipers smearing the first few drops of rain around on the glass. The trees on the right-hand side of the road, lit by headlights, were smeared a little from being captured in mid-motion. On the left was a dark space with a few trees. Droplets of rain on the hood were highlighted with yellow half-moons.

I said, "What is that?"

"Maddy has the video from my dash cam," Bob said. It almost didn't sound like his voice. He reached down and took the flask out of his pants pocket and drank from it, finishing it off with long, noisy gulps. "It shows...I can play it."

"No," Maddy said from the other side of the room.

"Yes," I said. "Play it."

Bob shuddered. He reached across the keyboard and clicked the mouse.

The trees on the right and the rocks on the left-hand side of the screen moved toward us, at too high a speed. It was raining and the trees were rocking as if the wind were whipping them. There was no sound. The truck drifted across the median as the curve tightened, wandering into the other lane.

The lights on the droplets changed angles as someone came around the corner in front of the truck.

The oncoming vehicle had only a single headlight.

The vehicle—the motorcycle—swerved and so did the truck, the view jumping in front of us. The truck sped up, jumping forward toward the motorcycle.

"I hit the gas," Bob said. "I meant..."

He stopped talking. I didn't care what he'd meant.

The headlight of the motorcycle swerved even more sharply and turned sideways, the wheels skidding on the wet asphalt. I caught a glimpse of Jack's helmet. I knew it was his because of the unmistakable longhorn skull on the side.

Then he was sliding off the road. He hit the side rail and went over, disappearing between a pair of trees.

I had seen the end results of that crash; they haunted my dreams. I didn't bother to imagine them then. I'd be seeing them again as soon as I closed my eyes, when I finally fell asleep. I watched the video.

The truck kept driving. It swerved again. I saw a dark flash across the window, reflected movement from inside the truck cab.

Then the screen went dark, the video stopped, and Bob looked up.

"You killed him," I said.

He looked like the victim of a vampire in a movie. He was pale and shaking, dripping with sweat. He put his hand down to the flask again, took it out, shook it, and tossed it to Tony.

"Yes," he said. He didn't apologize. He didn't tell me how sorry he was. He didn't offer to turn himself in to the cops. The grimace on his face was too profound for me to doubt his feelings. I accepted them.

I turned back toward Jim.

"And you," I said. "What did you do? Cut his brakes?"

Nick said, "He tightened the cable tension on the rear brake. Not enough to make it undrivable. Just enough to make it less responsive."

Something inside me moved, a curious flopping feeling, as though a coiled snake had suddenly turned over in its sleep.

"You didn't kill my husband," I told Jim. "You just played the odds. You got in a fight with Jack. And then you just played the odds. You don't need to win every hand. You just need to win often enough. What was it? What did he do to you?"

Jim didn't answer.

Marianne did.

"Jim wanted to buy the business," Marianne said. "He wanted to buy the business and hire Jack back on as an employee."

I laughed. "You probably told him he had insufficient capital to take advantage of the market and that you'd be doing him a favor. That he had to support his wife the writer, who would never make enough money to follow her dream."

From the look on Jim's face—which didn't change—I didn't think I was wrong. He certainly didn't bother to deny it.

I said, "And then Jack laughed at you. You killed my husband because he told you no."

I hadn't raised my voice the entire time. Jim hadn't backed down. He hadn't lowered his eyes. He hadn't expressed any shame, any reduction, any reversal. Any change. I wonder what I would have done if he had. If he'd have said something like, "But I didn't mean it," would it have changed anything? I feel like he would have died with a scoring pencil through his throat if he had said anything at that moment, but maybe he wouldn't have. We were surrounded by people, including four boys whose only involvement in all of this was to carry out Maddy's every whim:

they could have stopped me, after all, if Maddy had wanted to save me from myself.

Jim stood there, wrapped in arrogance.

Invulnerable.

In fact, he was shaking—not with fear, he didn't have enough humanity for that—but with anger.

Marianne said, "I'm leaving you, Jim. It's over. I've already gone into your emails and forwarded everything to Maddy and Sally."

Jim's lips pulled back, showing teeth that looked yellow in the living room lights.

Tony and Austin were behind him. The writer in me wanted to see Jim suddenly stiffen, his sneer turn into a grimace of pain, and—I don't know—the tip of a knife emerge from between his ribs, soaking his shirt in slowly seeping blood for a moment before he collapsed.

However, the writer in me had also been indulging in revenge fantasies for a year. The quick death was a fantasy that passed relatively quickly: this was Maddy's house.

Maddy had to be protected.

And Marianne.

And even Sally.

And...Bob. God help him, he owed me a favor now. More than a favor.

I looked at Bob and said, "You owe me a life."

"I owe you a life," he said, voice shaking and still sounding like it was someone else speaking.

That meant all my loose ends were tied up.

All that was left was Jim.

More sure of myself now, I said, "Go home, Jim. The police will be contacting you in the morning."

"I'll have you all charged—"

I stood off the stool and shook Wendy's hand away from mine. I walked up to him. I wasn't much shorter than he was, but suddenly I was looking straight into his eyes.

Then I was looking down at him.

"I'm taking your life, Jim Griffiths," I said. "And there is nobody who will stop me. Your wife is leaving you, Bob and Tony will cover up the trail of digital evidence for us, and Sally will give us blackmail material to use against you. I'm sure we can find a couple of friendly lawyers to blacken your name before we even go to trial. Everything that was yours is now *mine*."

"You're crazy!"

I reached out and put a hand on the side of his neck, pressing hard on the carotid sinus baroreceptor. All that research and this was the payoff: worth it. He swayed.

"Nothing I do to you matters," I said, pressing harder. His eyes went a little glassy. "Nothing you do matters at all."

He swung his hands at me then, shouting. I knew he would. Underneath all of his posturing, there was no rational thought, only animal reactions. Bristling fur. Territorialism. A bear's growl. I stepped out of the way and Tony and Austin grabbed his arms. It was like watching a well-planned chess move. Nick moved Maddy out of the hall and Egan disappeared down the hall. The back door opened. Tony and Austin dragged Jim toward the door. He was outside before he could get another breath.

I followed him.

It had started pouring again. Egan had slipped in through the side door of the garage and was raising the roll-up front door. Light spilled out of the garage, into the heavy rain. The last fragments of hail were melting on the gravel. They crunched underfoot like tiny skulls.

The two boys dragged Jim through the front door of the garage. Jim's bike was sitting there, waiting. They hoisted him up and dropped him, straddling, onto its seat.

Everything human about Jim was gone. His well-groomed gray hair stuck out in every direction. His face was alternately splotched and pale, like a moving Rorschach blob under the skin. His hands were as twisted and gnarled as claws, his squared-off fingernails trying to gouge the boys' eyes out as he struggled with them. His clothes were rumpled: polo shirt and khakis were hanging on him at odd angles. His eyes were insane, rolling and bulging from his head. His lips were white, whiter than his yellow teeth. His tongue was bright red. He'd bitten it. A trail of blood ran out of the corner of one side of his mouth.

"Goodbye, Jim," I said, slowly raising a hand. I was invoking ancient gods—or goddesses—of vengeance. "Drive safe."

As if he were on autopilot, he started the engine. "You'll hear from my lawyer!"

Without looking at any of us, he sped out of the garage, kicking up gravel as he hit the road. His red taillights swept, too fast, around the corner with the boulder, and disappeared into the night.

THE REST OF THE STORY

And now for the rest of the story, as Paul Harvey used to say on the radio when I was a kid.

We left Jim's punishment to the fates.

Later we found out that Jim had called his lawyer, saying only that he wanted to meet with him the following day; Marianne was planning to divorce him, and he wanted to make sure that she didn't walk away with a single blood-red cent. He'd somehow made it down to Evergreen Lake before calling—exactly the wrong direction he had needed to take in order to make it home.

Was he trying to get as far away as possible before daylight hit him? Was he trying to reach someone in particular?

Maddy's theory is that he was trying to make it to a woman's house, someone he was sleeping with. Sally agreed with her and threw out several names that I didn't recognize. I felt relieved. For some reason, I had been worried that Jim had been sleeping with someone I knew. I'd never be able to look at them without contempt again. I could understand someone getting pulled into the dank vortex that was Jim Griffiths, but I couldn't imagine having known what he was like, at least on the neighborhood gossip level, and *then* sleeping with him.

The three of us did not discuss the matter with Marianne, who went back to using her maiden name, Rael, as soon as the funeral was over.

After leaving the voice mail with his lawyer, Jim kept driving. He made it an incredible distance that night, considering that the storm was still rolling through the mountains until after sunrise the next morning, and the fact that the boys had done to Jim's bike what he had done to my husband's.

(I had asked them later how they had known what Jim had done, and they'd said they hadn't actually known for sure. They'd just guessed—and Jim hadn't denied it.)

Jim went off the road on Pine Valley Road, south of Evergreen, south of the entire Denver Metro area, south of Conifer and Aspen Park. The highway was a nice drive to get to Deckers or Woodland Park. It was nowhere near where Jack had died, for which I was glad. There was a sharp turn to the left, and then another to the right. In between the two was a sharp dropoff, and a dent in the guard rail where a truck had hit it the previous week.

Jim had been driving too fast. He hit a patch of wet gravel on the road, slid into the guard rail, hit the dent in the guard rail, and went over.

Nobody found, or even suspected, any evidence that would have shown that his bike had been tampered with. We didn't say anything about the burglaries. Bob hadn't because he'd blamed himself for the failure of the security system. Sally hadn't because she'd spotted Nick in the neighborhood, the days that the burglaries had happened, and had a feeling that something was up (either that, or she had reasons of her own). Jim had called in the burglary to the police, but then Marianne had called back and said that it wasn't a burglary after all, but a bear.

Marianne hadn't originally been part of Maddy's plans. Or at least, that's what Maddy said.

I asked Marianne about it, at the funeral.

Marianne looked completely different. I was surprised but not shocked. Jim's relatives seemed to take her for granted, commenting on her haircut and style change as "finally acting her age," but not surprised; Marianne's relatives seemed deeply shocked, yet pleased.

She had cut her long, dyed-red hair back to a pixie cut and turned it to a silvery gray that wasn't quite natural (not that quickly!), but a pleasing sort of silver-fox color. She had changed her makeup, getting rid of most of it. All that was left was a little bit of a smoky eye and some red lipstick, as far as I could tell. Very Helen Mirren-esque.

She wore a simple black sheath that went down to her calves and covered her wrists, not a single detail on it. It was like a television screen that has suddenly gone dark. Her chest was flatter than I remembered. I wondered if she'd been padding her bra all those years, and had finally been able to stop. She looked good.

She shook hands and looked tired and sad until she spoke with her relatives, who shook their heads at her and looked incredulous. She smiled when she saw them, a genuine smile although exhausted. I'm not a lip reader, but I think I saw her mouth the word "o-ver" several times while talking to them.

Finally I caught her alone for a few moments. I hadn't seen her since that night, not because she was avoiding me, but because, as I knew, funerals are busy times.

Even if you're not exactly grieving.

"Marianne," I said, shaking her hand, surprised at the callouses on the skin. "My sympathies. This must be a very trying time for you."

"It is," she said.

"Nice haircut," I added.

She gave me a flash of a smile. "I hear the writing is going well."

"It is," I said. "I'm writing two books at once, actually—the one to finish up a contract, and the other to please myself."

Her smile widened. "I know the feeling."

I looked around; nobody, finally, was within listening distance. "Bears?" I asked.

She blinked at me, not understanding, then laughed. "Yes, that was Jim all over, wasn't it? To be so paranoid and self-important to think that a break-in was an attack against him personally, when all that happened was a few trash cans had been tipped over and his papers dragged all over the yard. I *told* him that he needed to buy a shredder."

It was a good story. False, I knew, but she delivered it so well that I almost believed her.

Then she winked.

"Did you know?" I asked. "What Maddy had planned."

She shook her head, still smiling.

And then she said, "I had no idea, I just wanted to frustrate Jim. I've always had a feeling about Maddy, though."

"What?"

"That this isn't the first time she's done something like this."

And with that, she excused herself and rejoined a group of Jim's expensively dressed relatives, who eyed her perfect black gown with disdain as she accepted a glass of white wine.

A funeral was not the place to stain your teeth by drinking a red, after all.

———

Bob waved at me every time he saw me around, and I waved back. Neither one of us had forgotten what he owed me, but it wasn't the kind of thing that should come up in casual conversation. "Hey, Bob, how are you? Are you taking care of yourself? You better be, because your whole life belongs to me," isn't something you want to joke about in the grocery store. But I heard from the grapevine (i.e., Sally) that he had gone to AA and had burst out laughing at the part when they told him he had to give himself to a higher power.

They asked him what was so funny—was he an atheist or something?

He'd said something like, "I used to be," and laughed even harder.

I don't think of myself as particularly terrifying (or as a higher power). But he has his five-month coin now.

Bob isn't avoiding me, but Sally is. I'm not sure what that's all about. It's subtle. If I show up somewhere that she is and spot her, she'll come over and ask me how the writing is going. But I've heard one too many stories of how "you just missed her!" to think that it's a coincidence.

She has never since joked about me being naïve, though. I think that must be connected somehow.

Nick and the boys went back down to Denver. Nick got back together with the ex against Maddy's not especially strongly expressed wishes—"Let him amuse himself," she'd said, "that woman will never understand the difference between being flattered and being cared for"—and continued to wait on Maddy hand and foot. Maddy caught pneumonia the following winter and had to be taken to the hospital; I watched the house while she was gone. I spent the time looking for the other half of the secret basement, but it was no good. I found nothing. Maybe I'd imagined it all; maybe she'd left the room before Marianne and stepped into the bathroom and I hadn't seen her.

Maybe.

What I did notice about the house was that it held a suspicious dearth of personal items. The bedroom was much less feminine, for example, although what *that* meant, I had no idea.

I took Jack's tattooed skull home one night. I'd left it under the sheet in the guest room for several weeks at that point. I was writing a lot, and I could barely remember to eat, let alone notice that the skull wasn't where it was supposed to be.

In exchange I left a lithograph from a trip to Taos that Jack and I had bought and hung in the living room

The lithograph shows three cowgirls standing next to each other, smiling. One of them is wearing a cowboy hat and a fringed denim shirt. The middle one is wearing a red shirt and an old-fashioned women's Western tie, more of a scarf than anything else. She has an open expression. The one on the right is wearing a white shirt and the same kind of tie, her hair back in a chignon. You can tell at a glance that she's the sarcastic one. It's all in the sharpness of her laugh lines.

Above them is a red-winged blackbird sitting on some autumn brush, almost leafless. The blackbird looks as though it's bleeding at the breast, but it isn't.

I *liked* that picture.

But I also knew that Maddy was the one who ought to have it.

When Nick finally brought her back from Denver—it seemed to take forever, everyone on tenterhooks, not saying what they feared, that at her age she wouldn't be back—she settled into her house with great contentment.

I was, of course, invited over for coffee the very next day. Wendy was there; she'd been upgraded from "house cleaner" to "factotum," running all Maddy's errands and making sure she stuck to her doctor's prescribed diet—most of the time.

Wendy was as reticent as ever, but seemed to share a warmth with me out of the corners of her eyes, as it were. I felt—this is strange—that the two of us were related somehow. I'd been upgraded from a reasonably decent acquaintance to some sort of second cousin. Maybe it was just that our loyalties lay with Maddy, although it didn't feel like that was all of it.

Wendy served us coffee with too much cream, and goat cheese with red-pepper jelly on little crackers. Simple; delicious. And probably all kinds of forbidden for Maddy.

"So you didn't find it," Maddy said as we sat at the table.

"Nope," I said.

There was no point in pretending that I didn't know what she was talking about: the other half of the secret basement. Or, worse, that Wendy knew about it when I didn't!

I said, "Looking for it made me think about what you were doing, though. First, there was a secret when I had no idea there was anything to hide. Then there was another secret—hidden by the first secret. When I thought about what you were doing, I still didn't get it, but it kind of put me in the right frame of mind to accept it when I did find out. Luring me over here with the burglary was the first secret—but my husband's death was the second."

"Oh, good," Maddy said. "I didn't plan for you to find out that way, but I'm glad."

"You were going to accuse me of the burglaries, let me prove that I didn't do it, then let me put together the clues to solve the mystery that it was you, and that you'd done it to find out who'd killed Jack."

"Something like that," she said. "I suspected something was up when Jim was affected by Jack's death. Then Sally said something about Jim deciding to pay your house a call, and I decided to have the boys do a little research for me."

"Thank you," I said. "I was starting to go crazy. I was obsessed with revenge. The nightmares were killing me."

Maddy gave me a small, half-suppressed smile. "You were starting to figure it out on your own. And your instincts were taking over. I was terrified over the week before the party that you *would* figure it out, and decide to do something on your own."

I remembered what Marianne had said at the funeral, that Maddy had done something like this before. I decided not to ask.

"Did you plan out his death?"

"I planned out justice," Maddy said. "He *could* have stayed the night. Surrounded by angry women and big, burly boys who would beat the shit out of him at a word for me. He *could* have gone straight home."

She took my hand.

"You mustn't feel guilty about this," she said, clearly concerned.

"I don't!" I laughed. "That's what worries me most, Maddy. Everything fit together like it was fated. Even the storm. The heavens themselves were cooperating with you."

Maddy murmured, "Sometimes it does seem that way," and changed the subject.

We discussed the painting I had given her, an upcoming informal post-Christmas party, a play that had been put on by the local high school (*Arsenic and Old Lace*), the best brands of gin.

Small talk.

Maddy became short-tempered and I excused myself. Time to go. On my way out, Wendy gave me a hug that made me feel like I'd gone from second-cousin once removed to first cousin without knowing it. I told Maddy that I'd see her soon, and she said to get the hell out of her house, didn't I have a home to go to?

I went home and worked on the second book I was working on, the book of my heart, deep into the midnight hours.

Where it would lead me and my career, I had no idea. It was a darker story, less comfortable. My agent wasn't sure about the idea. A couple of my writer friends had read the opening, and they weren't sure about it, either.

The wind blew, scattering snow over the mountain. The hard flakes rattled on the windows.

Unused gifts turn to poison, I told myself, and thought fondly of my friend Maddy.

Author Checkin!

Hi all!

I'm writing this the day after the service of my friend (and author) Travis Heerman. It was held at the Denver Zen Center. I attended over Zoom and wept my eyes out, laughed too. That was the kind of guy he was. One of the readings was from *Fahrenheit 451*; another a poem by Marichiko. A friend (Thea Hutcheson) told a story about him being the "body" in a murder mystery party game; he'd whispered to her that he'd tell her everything he knew if she gave him five dollars. She did, and he answered: "THEA! I'M DEAD!" At the service, she ended the story with, "And for a moment, only a moment, I wished he *were* dead. But now I don't." And to me, that perfectly encapsulated Travis, and Thea too.

I knew him because I'd edited him for the anthology series Amazing Monster Tales, and because he, Jamie Ferguson, Rebecca Hodgkins, and I did a few meetings for brainstorming indie writer marketing things (and keeping each other motivated) right before Covid hit. He was kind when he didn't have to be, treated me with respect when I was struggling to do the same, and listened. He rambled, too, and was frustrated that his career wasn't where he wanted it to be, and anyone who read his stories knew he had darkness in him, too, lots of anger. But however dark it was inside him, he used it to bring support and understanding and humor to others.

And that is something I hope to carry forward myself.

———

Per Travis's family, if you knew him:

In lieu of flowers, the family is requesting donations in Travis' memory to Odyssey Writing Workshops. https://www.odysseywo rkshop.org/support-us/The simplest ways to donate are to send a check to Odyssey, P.O. Box 75, Mont Vernon, NH 03057, or go to https://paypal.com and send the donation to jcavelos@odyssey workshop.org. Please include Travis' name on your check or in the notes section on Paypal, so they will know it's for his memorial.

———

A Dark and Cozy Night was written in 2019 off and on while I was still ghostwriting, before I got sick with something very like Covid after the MileHi Con in Denver in October (that kept me conked out until March, when Actual Covid hit), before the big split with my ex in May 2020. I finished it put it in a back drawer in my mind and didn't think about it. At the time I had this feeling that I knew how to write cozy mysteries as a ghostwriter, but I didn't know how to write them as myself, and I wanted to see if I could find a good compromise. I felt like I'd failed, like the manuscript needed ten thousand changes.

The series (it's a series) started with another book called *The Second Cabin* that I want to completely tear apart and rewrite and use a different title for. It's about a writers' retreat in the mountains; a lot of the ideas that are in *A Dark & Cozy Night* came from *The Second Cabin*, but they're better done here. (Mostly I just want to preserve the setting and characters and use a different plot.) I wrote *The Second Cabin* in early 2016, right around the same time that I started having to defend myself from people I thought of as family and close friends over politics. It wasn't *always* my conservative connections, but it was *mostly* my white, male conservative friends. Liz Hicks comes out of that place: finding out that people who called themselves family and friends were perfectly willing to harass me—even sexually harass me—erase my opinions, invalidate me personally and professionally, and then tell me I was being divisive when I resisted the process of being shaped into a mindless drone. A lot of the people were other writers, people I admired for their keen critical eye.

Naively, I had been shocked.

Didn't friendship mean that others could at least take on a "live and let live" policy, the way I had been for years? Couldn't we just agree to disagree? Apparently not.

Since then I've learned to tap into the more ruthless aspects of myself, clearly inherited along both sides of my family, and don't hesitate to give "friends" the boot (or at least a block) when I'm sure that they would rather behave unethically than be wrong. The better boundaries I set, the more clear it is who's worth keeping as a friend and who isn't. I *know* what happens when I try to make things work: I get drained and I end up distrusting everyone around me. The decision to remove someone from my life is easier now.

But at the time I felt naked rage.

I'd spent most of my life suppressing anger, letting it out in a few horror stories, but mostly keeping a tight rein on it, lest I turn into the people who bullied me. It turns out that keeping anger locked up tight is just as destructive as barfing it all over the place. Liz is where I first started exploring the idea that there could be positive ways to use anger, positive ways to use one's darker side.

The Second Cabin is later in the series. This one's just where it starts.

A Dark & Cozy Night isn't *really* a cozy mystery. But, looking back over it, it's something I'm proud that I wrote, even if it doesn't quite fit.

I hope that if you're struggling with anger that you can find something in Maddy (if not yet Liz) that helps settle things a bit. People say "we all have a dark side," but it's not *quite* true. We all have a side of ourselves that we would rather not acknowledge, it's true, but sometimes the nicest people are also the ones gripping down the hardest to make sure none of that darkness spills out.

(Okay, maybe they'll let themselves have a little sarcasm, as a treat.)

That darkness can be a gift, but WOW is it hard to learn how to use safely.

That's what I'm exploring with Liz. I hope it helps and you enjoy it.

Love, De

Tampa, Florida
May 18, 2024

Acknowledgements

You know what, this book is for all the writers I'm still friends with. It has been a wild ride since 2016. In particular, I want to thank MB Partlow, Shannon Lawrence, Veronica Callisto, and Sue Mitchell, who particularly inspired me around the time the earlier (unpublished) book in this series was written, during the lead-up to the 2016 US presidential elections. Y'all are not *nice* but you are all wickedly funny and I was inspired. Thank you.

Thanks to my editor, Alicia, even if I put you through hell!

I think Trav would have liked this one. Even better, he might have argued with me about it.

As always, for Ray.

More To Read!

Your Soufflé Must Die

If you enjoyed this story, please consider checking out *Your Soufflé Must Die.*

Nobody delivers savory, surprising fiction quite like DeAnna Knippling, author of 80+ books.

Sam's Colorado kitchen at three a.m.: burnt chocolate on the counter, cold coffee going colder, crude capitals mocking her first in-person cooking class from her laptop screen:

YOUR SOUFFLE MUST DIE LOL.

Who would write such a thing?!?

Some stupid Internet troll who knows her schedule. Someone who knows the menu. Someone who knows enough to threaten her desserts.

Sam runs Sweet Granadilla Catering alone - every spectacular disaster, every delicious triumph. Now someone wants to sabotage her desserts and prove her wrong.

But NOBODY threatens Sam's desserts and gets away with it.

A wicked, clever cozy mystery about sabotage, desserts, and going it alone until you can't.

—*Your Soufflé Must Die* came out of the question: what if the crime involved wasn't murder? Would it still work as a cozy mystery? I wrote this book while also writing a bunch of cozy mystery novels for ghostwriting clients. The books they wanted had normal, nice, sane people as chefs and cooks and caterers...which, if you've ever worked in the food industry, you know is *not* realistic.

You can find it via my website <u>wonderlandpress.com</u>.

YOUR SOUFFLÉ MUST DIE

Sam stared at the screen in disbelief. She couldn't hear a sound, and someone had sucked all the air out of the room while simultaneously replacing it with ice.

YOUR SOUFFLE MUST DIE, DEC 3 LOL.

Someone, some horrible internet troll, had left a comment on her latest post on her website, FoodSlutOnline.com. Horrible internet trolls had happened to her before, but she'd always had Harry to deal with them.

But her problems were no longer Harry's problems, and she had no intention of calling him to ask what to do about a rude comment on her website.

Someone was making death threats on her cooking. And *LOL*. Honestly. It wasn't funny.

She wished the comment would just go away, then suddenly realized that it could, if she wanted it to. Her mouse pointer hovered over the Trash button for a second. What if she needed it later? What if the troll sent another comment, just like it? What if they murdered her soufflé and she needed evidence for the police?

Okay. Time to stop going off the deep end, Sam. That's exactly the kind of comment from you that would start a fight with Harry. Keep thinking things like that, and you're going to prove him right: You're a spaz. Six months without him, and your bank accounts are going to be a shambles, your site will close down, and your new catering business will fail!

Sam sighed, leaned back in her computer chair, and rubbed her eyes. Clearly, this was not a night to be alone. She turned off her computer monitor and the banker's lamp over Granny's roll-top desk, then padded downstairs in her sweatpants to call Kaley.

The house phone was downstairs on the far side of the kitchen, where she could pretend she couldn't hear it ringing if she didn't feel like answering. She picked up the handset, dialed Kaley's number from memory, and waited. First ring, second ring...

Kaley's mom answered. "Hello? Lugano residence. Marilyn speaking."

"Hi, Marilyn," Sam said, dancing from foot to foot on the cold tile. "Is Kaley home?" She felt like she was twelve again, instead of thirty-three.

"She is, dear. Would you like to speak to her?"

"If you please." Sam giggled as Marilyn dropped the phone on the counter and yelled her daughter's name at the top of her voice.

Kaley shouted back, "Got it!" and picked up the upstairs phone. Sam never called Kaley on her cell phone at home. The sheer drama and politics of family members answering each others' calls was just too funny.

"Yeah?" she said.

"Aren't you going to ask who it is?"

"I already know who it is," Kaley said. "What do you want?"

"If you ask your mom if you can have a sleepover at my house, do you think she'll be mad?"

Kaley snorted like a pig over the phone. "God, you're such a twit."

Sam laughed. "I promise I won't get you drunk and fat."

Kaley blew air across the phone, and it hissed in Sam's ear. "Nervous about tomorrow?"

"No, I mean yes, some douchebag left a comment on Food Slut threatening my soufflés tomorrow."

"How did they know that?"

"What?"

"That the soufflé class was tomorrow? You didn't announce the date change."

"Oh, that's true. I just sent out an email to the class." Sam paced back and forth through the kitchen, running one hand across her countertops and her new marble slab for chocolate and a butcher's block in the center island. "Hm...I don't know."

"Did you ask Harry about it?"

"When you get divorced, that means that the other person doesn't want you to come running to them with all your problems anymore, Kaley."

"Yeah, but death threats on your desserts."

Sam wanted to laugh it off, but she couldn't. "So come over? We can watch something out of Jack Malpeque's *oeuvre* and try out the winter aphrodisiac nibbles for next month's class."

Kaley squealed. "The truffles came in?"

"No, sorry. We're just going to have to use the frozen truffles."

"When are they coming in?"

"Monday. Supposedly." Three days away; an eternity, as far as she was concerned. "I'll throw in some chai vodka."

"Deal." The phone beeped off, and Sam went back upstairs, turned on her monitor, and looked at the comment again.

She had no idea how to tell who it was from. She pasted the email address into a search engine; all that came back was that the address belonged to a remailer, which was (she looked it up) a service that took off your real address and replaced it with another one. It sounded like something that even Harry would have trouble with. Weird. One, why bother making empty threats on her soufflés? Two, why bother going through all the secrecy? Usually trolls didn't bother hiding their identity too hard. They usually just wanted to yell at her for trying to make cooking funny and sexy instead of too complex and boring to bother with.

She usually got comments that boiled down to *What's the point of making delicious food if it isn't hard?* And *Why do you have to make so many jokes about sex?* Which always struck her as pretty stupid.

She turned off the monitor again, went into the back pantry and started pulling down ingredients. Raw avocado-chocolate pudding: avocados, cocoa powder, agave, sea salt, vanilla...Figs and chorizo: dried figs, Spanish sausage, pimentón, cinnamon, Manzanilla sherry, olive oil...Truffled ravioli: fontina, dried truffles, honey, pears, and walnuts... She stopped. She couldn't remember what the last dish was.

Ah. Shrimp bisque. Harry's favorite.

When the doorbell rang, she dumped everything on the counter, sniffed back tears, and opened the door for Kaley.

"Cutting onions?" Kaley asked.

She shook her head. "Shrimp bisque."

Kaley dumped her bag on the floor and hugged her, then stepped in out of the cold. "Poor thing. You should take it off the menu."

"No...it's perfect," she hiccupped. "I can't tell you the number of times he dragged me to bed after I made him shrimp bisque. It works. I have to move on."

Kaley shook her head at her. "Now you know why I never married."

"You just haven't met the right man yet."

Kaley rolled her eyes. "I have met the right man. He's just married and a professional hockey player. Oh, yeah. And I've never actually met him."

"He signed your jersey." But Sam was feeling better, wiping her face on a tissue, leading Kaley back into the kitchen.

"He signs everyone's jerseys. Ooh, we're going with the pudding? I don't know about that. Raw food. It just sounds like it's for a bunch of weirdos. I don't know if anyone will try it."

"We'll give them some first and then explain how to make it. They won't know what hit them." Sam checked the avocadoes, which were hefty, full, and with just a little give under her fingers. "So rich...so delicious." She stroked the avocado suggestively. "So...*ahuacate*."

But she had already shocked Kaley with her explanation of the Aztec word for avocado (testicle), and Kaley, whose eyes must be in a perpetual state of dizziness from rolling at Sam's bad jokes all the time, ignored her and went straight for the freezer. "I believe I was promised chai vodka."

They worked on the appetizers for half an hour before Sam remembered the reason she'd asked Kaley to come over. "Oh!

I almost forgot. That stupid threat on the soufflés. Would you help me check the kitchen? I want to make sure there aren't any booby traps or anything like that."

"Paranoid much?"

"You know me."

They searched the kitchen, checking the eggs and the other ingredients, looking over the guest list for any possible saboteurs, and discussing the possibility of whether a truck with a super-loud stereo parked on the street could knock over a soufflé: Sam for, Kaley against. Colorado Springs seemed to have become a haven for giant trucks over the last decade.

"Anyone who had to park on the street would be blocked by the house, Sam. He might rattle windows on the west side in the living room, but there's no way the sound could make it all the way back here, not loud enough to knock over a soufflé."

Sam shook her head, waving her short blonde pigtails back and forth. "This is our first class, Kaley. I'm so nervous I could almost puke. I just know this is going to be a failure. Like Harry always said—"

"—Nobody trusts a skinny cook," Kaley finished for her. "Honestly. Could you just have a little faith in me for a while, even if you don't trust yourself? If the company falls flat, it's as much my fault as it is yours."

"Sorry."

"And don't give me that puppy-dog look, either. Save it for your gentlemen callers."

Sam snorted. "And who might those be?"

"You're doing better than me. The only man under the age of sixty-five who's been in my house for the last six weeks is Dale."

Sam laughed, then said, "How are things going with him?" Dale was Kaley's older brother, an electrical engineer at a computer hardware company.

"He's..."

"Do you think you can still work with him, if we need to hire him to help with catering? He's been asking. But if you don't want him to be around, I'll tell him no. I won't explain why or anything. Or I could lie."

"You shouldn't lie to people anymore. You say the craziest shit. No wonder nobody believes you. No, I can work with him, I just can't talk to him about mom and dad and the garage."

"Neither one of you knows anything about cars. You should just sell it and split the profits. After your parents pass on."

"He still thinks he should inherit the whole thing. So he can run it into the ground, I guess. He thinks it's his ticket out of a desk job. After all, if *you* can run a business, why can't he?"

Sam sighed. "He shouldn't take me as an example. It just kind of fell into my lap."

"Don't be silly. All right, I think we've checked everything we can check."

Sam took off the lid of the pot where the shrimp stock was simmering. "I think we're good, here." She reached out for her fine-mesh strainer from its hook overhead and swiped her hand through nothing but air. "Oh, I forgot. It's out in the garage. Harry took it with him by mistake and brought it back a few days ago. I'll be right back."

She went into the garage, swinging her arm around through the dark for the cord overhead. She hit it so hard that the cord popped away from her hand and she had to wait a moment for it to come back to her.

She pulled the cord. For a second, the light flashed brightly, casting shadows all over the garage, and she thought she saw something moving around behind her SUV.

Just then, Kaley screamed and something that sounded as loud as a gunshot cracked out from the kitchen.

...

You can find *Your Soufflé Must Die* via my website: <u>wonderlandpress.com</u>

About the Author

DeAnna Knippling is a versatile author celebrated for her imaginative storytelling across multiple genres, including gothic horror, steampunk, puzzle mystery, psychological suspense, and dark fantasy. Her works, such as *The House Without a Summer* and *The Clockwork Alice*, have garnered praise for their inventive narratives and unique twists on classic tales. Readers commend her ability to blend the macabre with the whimsical, creating immersive worlds that captivate and intrigue. Whether exploring twisted fairytales or unraveling crime, DeAnna's stories linger long after the final page. Find her at WonderlandPress.com.